GOTTIKA

GOTTIKA

Helaine Becker

Illustrations by
Vero Navarro

Green
Bean
Books

Green
Bean
Books

First published in 2021 by Green Bean Books,
c/o Pen & Sword Books Ltd,
47 Church Street, Barnsley, S. Yorkshire, S70 2AS
www.greenbeanbooks.com

© Helaine Becker 2021
Illustrations © Vero Navarro

ISBN 978-1-78438-575-0
Harold Grinspoon Foundation edition ISBN 978-1-78438-579-8

Library of Congress Cataloging-in Publication Data available

Typeset by JCS Publishing Services Ltd, www.jcs-publishing.co.uk
Printed and bound by CPI Group (UK) Ltd, Croydon, CR0 4YY

The thing I don't like about being a kid is this:

Adults lie to us.

They don't want to scare us with the truth.

Instead, they tell us fairy stories, full of twinkly happily ever afters.

But kids know life isn't fair.

Believe me, we know.

Tomorrow I will leave my childhood behind.

Tomorrow, I will know the truth.

PART I

The holy voice from above went still. In its place, holy letters fell from the heavens into the hearts of those ready to heed them. But many ages have passed since such letters have fallen, and still more that the heavens have remained silent.

1

So you probably want to know a little bit about me.

My name is Dany and I'm an only child. But most of us Stoon kids were onlies. None of us was sure why.

We lived in Gottika. Or I suppose I should say, in the shadow-town of Gottika—the favela that had grown up on the southwest edge of the city. Its nickname was the Stews, because we just sat there and stewed, waiting for things to get better.

Inside the Stews, we were pretty much free to live how we wanted. Except for a few things. Like curfew.

> By order of Count Pol, the CURFEW will be 9 PM for all residents. NO EXCEPTIONS.
>
> Council Ruling #42.16, section III of the Gottikan District Code of Public Order. Subject to fines and/or punishment 100,000Gs/40 days Noathic Prison.

Another rule was that we all had to wear our *beretes*—our red Stoon hats—whenever we left the house. I didn't mind that. When you looked down from my room onto the market square, it was like gazing onto a field of poppies. Not that I'd ever seen real poppies. But it was what I imagined they'd look like. Bright and cheerful, like that.

My father was a scientist, philosopher, and healer. His study was on the top floor of our creaky house. You could almost always find him there, at his desk, surrounded by teetering piles of books, papers, and beakers with gunk at the bottom. His head turtled forward because of all the hours he spent bent over his work. He'd got a permanent squint, too, since he couldn't afford new reading glasses. But he didn't care about that. What he cared about was "advancing the cause of knowledge." If only he could get his stuff published again.

Here's how a typical conversation between my father and me went:

Me: Are you coming down to supper? We've got rice and beans tonight. Again.

Papa: I'll be down in a moment. As soon as I finish this thought.

Me: Riiiight. *(Sigh)*

My mother was a different story altogether. She suffered from what people around here called "the crying sickness."

In her case, the tears stopped falling when she stopped talking, so it was actually more like a staring sickness. Nowadays, she spent hours staring blindly at a piece of embroidery in her lap, one that hadn't had a new stitch added to it in months. Or she stared out the window, onto the market square. I don't think she imagined poppies there. I don't know what she saw.

A typical conversation with my mom went like this:

Me: Mom? Mom?
Mom: …
Me: *(Sigh)*

I suppose, in a way, you could say all three of us suffered from the staring sickness.

2

I already told you about the curfew. And the *beretes*.

But there were other rules for Stoons.

Like, we couldn't own pets.

We couldn't own land. No weapons either.

My father said it didn't matter that we didn't have guns. He was happier without them. "Why would we need them? We're a peaceful people," was his explanation.

What did matter to him was that since the time of the Troubles, we couldn't work as doctors or lawyers or professors in the University. And even worse, we could no longer practice magic.

I'll never forget the day the order came down.

My father, a copy of the announcement in his hand, paced like a madman. Two steps this way, two steps that, his progress blocked at every turn by precarious towers of books. He kicked one, and the books tumbled helter-skelter to the floor. He didn't notice. He tore at his hair and shouted, "It's pure nonsense!"

I clutched at him, I begged him to stop. But he was beyond hearing.

He slammed his fist on his worktable, again and again, making the writing utensils jump in their holder. "There's nothing 'sacrilegious' about it! Koper's solar system model or Gutenberger's mirror-writing machine—they're just tools. No different from hammers or wrenches! As if people don't already know that things fall down when you drop them!"

I was only a little kid back then, but I knew enough to be scared.

I knew that things break when they fall.

3

Things were all right for a while after that. But then, they got worse.

4

I stared at the naked shelves, unblinking. A lifetime of study, swept away.

"Can't we get them back, Papa?"

My father said nothing.

"Why can't we go to Count Rayn and ask him to help us get them back? You say he's been good to you before. You say he respects learning! Maybe he'll help with Count Pol!"

He drifted over to the window and thrust aside the drapes.

"Please, Papa! You have to do something!"

"It's too late. Even if Count Rayn dared to challenge Count Pol, it wouldn't make a difference. What's done is done."

He shifted his gaze. His shoulders sagged.

"But Papa! You can't just ... take it!"

He beckoned me over. "Look there. What do you see?"

I scanned the familiar scene below the window. "Nothing special. Just people milling about the market. But wait ... Today isn't market day ..."

I didn't understand the significance. I looked to my father for an explanation.

"Look harder, Dany. And remember the old proverb: The wise don't need eyes to see."

His words pricked my pride.

Fine. I'd show him.

I strained to see into the crowd.

At its center, a knot of ... soldiers. I couldn't see what they were doing.

I took a deep breath, and then another, in a vain attempt to slow my drumming heart.

That's when I caught the first whiff.

Smoke.

The soldiers were burning the books.

I flung myself away from the window.

My father wrapped his arms around me and held me tight to stop my shaking. His voice was calm. Soothing.

"Perhaps, when we can no longer make use of God's words here on Earth, it's fitting to return them to him."

5

That happened six months ago. A few weeks later, my best friend, Beano, needed to buy some clay to finish an art project. He was making a set of funny little marionettes for a children's play he·planned to put on at our community's midwinter carnival. Since clay was easier to get in Gottika proper than in the Stews—most everything was—we set out straight after school to make the trek.

Keeping our heads down, we scurried across Tian Square in front of Count Pol's residence. We both breathed easier when we reached the bustling shopping district on the other side.

"We have to hurry up," Beano said for the twelfth time. "You know my mom wants me back before sundown."

I barely heard him. A girl—a Gottikan girl—had caught my eye.

She was dressed like all her friends, in her school uniform. A plaid jumper over a white blouse, with navy knee-socks and a red necktie. But something about her, something you couldn't quite put your finger on, made her stand out like a red rose in a patch of thorns.

Maybe she felt my gaze on her. Maybe it was just one of those twists of fate. But suddenly she looked up. Her eyes met mine and she smiled.

Flustered, I turned away. She had so much confidence it unnerved me. She looked the way that I'd always imagined Princess Avivia would look if I ever saw her.

Beano was tugging at me. "Come on, Dany. We don't have all day, you know."

My feet were rooted to the spot. This girl seemed so sure of herself, so comfortable in her own skin—something I never felt anymore. I wanted to figure out how she did it.

Beano thwacked me on the head.

"For God's sake, D! What are you doing? Get a grip. C'mon! It's almost five!"

I knew Beano was right. We didn't have time to waste. Beano's mom was always sick with worry over him. As it was, we'd have to hurry if we were going to make it back to the Stews before sundown.

Beano was already on the move, threading his way through the crowd. Reluctantly, I turned my back on the girl and followed him.

The blow came as a complete shock. A solid *thunk* on the nape of my neck. Not painful, but certainly an attention-getter.

I raised my hand to the spot. Yanked it away again, fast, when I felt something cold there. Something slimy.

Mud, with a bit of horse turd in it.

Who did this? I'd show them! I'd give as good as I—

It was *her*. The Gottikan girl. The one who'd seemed so—together.

She was smirking, while all around her, her stupid friends shook with laughter.

Definitely not a princess.

I scraped the gross glob out of my hair as best I could and flung it to the ground. Some of it dribbled into my collar and snaked down my back.

I shouldered my way into the crowd and prayed for it to swallow me up. But I could still hear their laughter. That girl. *Those* girls. How I hated them!

I couldn't escape them, though. Even as the filth trickled down my spine, I knew I'd be lying awake for nights to come, reliving the humiliation.

6

A whisper rippled through the crowd.

Goose bumps rose on my arms. I stretched up onto my toes to see what was going on. There, at the far end of the street, was a closed black coach-and-four.

A gasp rose from fifty mouths at once.

"It's Pol!" someone said.

"The Count!" said another.

"Step lively if you know what's good for ya," a man with a gray cap said as he elbowed past me.

The dark coach hurtled closer. Coming straight for us.

Everyone drew together. It didn't matter, in that moment, if we were Stoons or Gottikans—we all had to come together, belly to belly, or risk getting trampled.

Not everyone made it to the safety of the circle. *She* was stuck with her friends on the other side of the road.

They looked terrified.

Of course they did. Those metal horses! Their alien screech of steel on steel chilled you to the core. Their cold flanks gleamed, and their chain-link manes glittered as they tossed their huge heads.

The four steel horses whinnied and reared. Sparks flew off the cobblestones. An ungodly noise blocked out all thought. I wanted to run, to run and never look back, but I was trapped. My heart thundered, my breath caught, my vision telescoped. A wall of hot wind struck me in the face. The coach screamed around the corner and was gone.

The crowd, like a single body, sagged in relief. One of the girls burst into tears.

Beano snickered. "They're not so high and mighty now, are they?"

My heart was still pounding in my ears, but I forced a grim laugh. "Yeah, well. Girls like that—any excuse for drama."

"Maybe. But they've got a pretty good excuse this time. We all do."

I snorted. "Like what?"

"You haven't heard? The Count's got a thing for 'traitors.' They say he goes around town scouting for enemies. Exactly like that—wearing his creepy metal mask and staring out of his creepy auto-coach." He flicked one hand toward where the coach had blasted past us. "That's why there've been so many disappearances lately."

"Yeah, right. And where did you hear this fairy tale?"

"*Everyone's* talking about it, Dany. And not just us Stoons."

"How do you know what the Gottikans are talking about? You got other connections I don't know? Like with girls who *don't* chuck turds at us?"

Beano's neck stiffened. "I get around. I keep my eyes open. And my ears. You should too, Dany, if you know what's good for you."

I raised an eyebrow at him. "Don't be such a sucker. There's no way Count Pol is kidnapping people. Especially Gottikans. *His own people*. Or should I say, 'The Golden Ones'?"

"No, really! He's nuts! He's like a madman or something."

At first I thought Beano was yanking my chain. But then I saw the fear in his eyes.

I glanced back at the girl.

Maybe her smile hadn't been phony. Maybe she'd just been scared—scared and pretending not to be. Like I was.

I tried to put the thought from my mind. We passed through an arched gateway into the covered market. On the other side lay a twisting labyrinth of arcades, each crammed with shops and every product imaginable. I must have looked ridiculous, head whipping this way and that, eyes trying to take in everything at once.

Beano didn't seem to notice the splendor around us. He was still caught up in his own inner vision.

"You can't deny it. There've been more than the normal amount of disappearances lately. Four just last month."

I puffed up my cheeks, then let the air out with a *pssshhh*. "That's business as usual in glorious, glorious Gottika. One day here, the next day—*pffft*."

Beano's eyes glazed over. "I wonder what it's like … when it happens."

I knew he was thinking about his father and sister. The rare, precious Stoon sib we all wanted, but few had.

"Like, you're just walking around, like we are now … And the next thing—*bammo*!" He slammed a clenched fist into his palm. "History," he whispered, as if I were no longer there to hear.

You see, Beano's mother wasn't the only one in his family with the worrying sickness.

7

We found the art supply stall without too much trouble—
Beano had been there before. It was an artist's dream
come true. Brushes, calligraphy pens, pads of paper and
canvases, jointed wooden models of human figures, little
dishes with ground pigments: all were piled high, in infinite
variety.

I had taken off my jacket and turned it inside out to
towel off my hair. It hadn't worked very well—I looked
like a sewer rat, and smelled worse. So I hung back as
Beano negotiated with the shopkeeper. I couldn't afford
any of the fancy pens and inks anyway, much as I would
have loved using them.

"I need a chunk about yay big." Beano drew the shape
and size of a brick in the air. "Medium grade."

The shopkeeper looked Beano up and down, up and
down. "Do you now? Fine. That'll be twelve gottikans."

Beano's voice rose, "But the sign says ten!"

The shopkeeper rested his beefy arms on the counter
and laughed. Not in a nice way, of course.

"Mebbe it does. But *I* said twelve gottikans. Take it or leave it, Stoon."

Beano's face went white. His lips went white too—a sign, I knew, that Beano was about to lose it. Beano had a low boiling point.

"B-b-but that's not fair! You've got a posted price of ten, so that's the—"

The shopkeeper stepped out from behind his counter. Got right into Beano's face. "Are your ears dirty, larv? Take it or leave it. *Larv*. Do you understand me?"

I didn't like where this was heading. This situation was just the type to set Beano's temper off. No one likes to be cheated. And being called a larv? Well, I wanted to plant my fist in that guy's face too.

A guard approached. He had a dog on a leash. A big dog. Beano's face paled even further.

I hissed into his ear, "Just pay for the stuff and let's get out of here."

Beano shifted from foot to foot, then plunked his twelve coins on the counter. "Okay! Okay! Just give it to me, then!" He slid the coins across the smooth wood. "Here."

The shopkeeper kept one eye on Beano as he counted them. Nice and slow, one by one. Then he checked them for legitimacy. One. By one. By one.

Beano's fidgeting intensified. He was not fond of the Militia. Or dogs.

The shopkeeper was finally satisfied. He reached under the counter and scrabbled around. Finally he came up with the cutting wire. Examined it. Ran the tip of his thumb and forefinger along it until the wire was completely straight. Once, and then again.

The guard drew closer.

The shopkeeper unwrapped the linen from the damp clay. With elaborate care, he lined up the clay against the wire.

Beano's foot tapped. He chewed on his thumbnail.

The guard's huge dog strained on its leash, snuffing everything in sight.

The wire came down.

Now the merchant only had to wrap the clay in waxed paper and say "thank you" to send us on our way.

Instead, he thrust the still-dripping clay into Beano's hands.

"Wrap is extra," he said with a thin, cold smile.

Beano spluttered. He bobbled the clay from hand to hand. I thought he might heave it right in the guy's mug.

The guard must have sensed something brewing. Suddenly he was at my side. His leashed monster snuffled at my shoes. Its hackles were up.

"Any problem here?"

"Uh, no. No, sir," Beano said, glowering.

"No," I said too.

The beast growled. My bones turned to water.

I didn't move a muscle. Not a twitch of my cheek. Not a flicker of my eyelid.

The guard grunted. "Better not be. We've had enough

23

trouble with your kind today. But, come to think of it, Dag and I wouldn't mind catching you out after curfew." He stroked the dog's head. "Right, Daggy boy?"

We wasted no time getting out of there.

8

I didn't see much of Beano for the next few weeks—he was always "busy." I figured he didn't want to talk about what had happened. I didn't either.

I missed hanging out with him, though. So one Sunday I made a point of meeting up with him at the corner café.

Beano had checked out a backgammon set from the barista and got us going on a fierce game as we sipped our hot cocolats. He rolled two fours and asked, "How are … things?" He wouldn't meet my eyes.

"Same as always. Like I'm always waiting for the other shoe to drop." I rolled a three and a four, hit two of his playing pieces, and set them on the bar between our sides. "You?"

"We've had big changes at our house," he said, after getting both of his men out of limbo with a roll of double sixes. "That's why I've been AWOL. Remember that guy from Praha who started hanging around my mom's market stall?"

"Yeah." Mrs. Beanburg's Jams & Jellies stall had been struggling lately.

"Well, Sandor and my mom … they discovered they have a lot in common. You know my mother never really recovered after the Militia arrested my father and took away my sister. I mean, my sister was, like, only a few days old. How do you get over something like that?"

I had no idea.

"Well, Sandor had it tough in Praha too," Beano continued. "His wife had the wasting disease. He kept making appointments to get her onto the radiation machines that could save her, but she kept getting bumped by Prahans! She got bumped so many times, she died before they got to her!"

"That sucks." I rolled a one and a four. That sucked too.

"As impossible as it sounds, Sandor and my mom hit it off. They're going to get married!"

My hand, holding the cup with the dice in it, froze. I searched Beano's face.

"No kidding! That's, uh, great … or is it? You okay with it?"

Beano waved his hand in the air and nodded. He took the cup and shook the dice.

"At first I felt awful. Guilty. And mad. Like—how can they be so happy? It's been a long time, but my father and sister are still, you know, *pffft*! I was afraid, too, because—hey, you know me, I always think if I let myself feel good about something, it will just get screwed up."

He threw the dice. Double sixes again.

"Whoa, today is your lucky day," I said with a grimace.

It looked like he'd be winning our backgammon game for sure.

"No joke. It feels like every day is my lucky day lately." He was looking past my shoulder and smiling like a goof.

I glanced around to see who it was that could turn Beano all googly like that.

Across the café was a girl I'd never seen before. She didn't go to school with us. And, believe me, every kid in the Stews our age went to school with us. So who was this girl, smiling back at Beano with a grin as wide as his?

"But that's not all," Beano was saying. He rose to his feet. "Sandor has a kid—a daughter! That means I'm going to have another *sib!*"

He held out his hand to the girl. "I asked her to come today. So you could meet her. And here she is. Dany, this is Ava. Ava, Dany."

My stomach did a double flip. I mumbled something inane about how nice it was to meet her, suddenly remembered "an errand I have to run for my dad," and got out of there quick as spit.

I was happy for my friend. Really, I was. But I was also jealous as all get-out. You see, I'd always wanted a sib.

9

"Blood. Then frogs. Then lice," goes the old proverb.

Do bad things really come in waves? It certainly seemed like it.

It was only a few days later that Beano came running up to me in the schoolyard. He was out of breath, and holding a special edition of the Stoon newspaper.

"Have you heard? Your cousin. Dalil. She's run off—in the middle of the night!"

A sick feeling washed over me. Dalil! In trouble!

Dalil was twenty-one, nine years older than me. She'd been my babysitter when I was little. Before my mother came down with the crying sickness.

Back then, I'd loved and feared Dalil in equal measure; she was beautiful and bossy and exciting and never followed the rules. Needless to say, Dalil was *way* more fun than anybody else, a hundred times more fun! With a magical flip of her hand, she could transform old socks into uber-realistic hand puppets. Her brilliant mimicry of the Elders—Raba-Caterina, Rob-Buda, and

Rob-Luria—would make me laugh so hard my stomach hurt. Yet Dalil's mood might instantly twist. Between one breath and the next she'd turn bitter and mean. She'd say something so cruel, so cutting, it would leave me reeling with shock and hurt.

But no matter what, she was my cousin. And I had few others. With so few Stoons having sibs, our family, like most others, was painfully small. Dalil was probably my tenth-cousin-twenty-times-removed, but it was easier just to say cousin.

I grabbed the newspaper from Beano's hand. Sure enough, Dalil was on the front page—her high-school graduation picture. She looked beautiful and beamy in it.

By the time I made it to the closest bench, my vision was going checkerboard. I put my head between my knees. It steadied me, but my forehead, my hands, still felt clammy.

Beano sank down beside me. "It says she was 'Chosen.' By Pol. That she's going to marry him!"

"But she's a Stoon! Why would Count Pol pick one of us for his wife? Isn't he the one that decided we're 'larvs'?"

"Isn't it obvious?" Beano said. "Beauty cancels out larv-hood." He groaned. "I still can't believe this is happening. It's just so … so … awful!"

"Yeah," I said, "her mom … she must be going crazy! And my father! He's going to throw a fit. I gotta get home."

"The final bell hasn't rung yet! You'll get demerits!" Beano called out after me.

♦

I found my father in the front hall. His shoulders drooped, and his face looked tired and thin. For the first time, he looked like an old man.

"So you've heard." He reached for his coat and *berete*.

"Where are you going?"

"Queen Areya is in Gottika, at the Autumn Palace. I'm going to request an audience."

I was stunned. What did he think *the Queen* could do?

I jammed my hands in my pockets. "Sure, Papa. That's a good one. It's not like you're gonna get an audience or anything. You're a *Stoon*. Remember?"

I expected my father's forehead to furrow and his jaw to tighten. He wasn't big on sass from me. But he didn't bite. He simply said, "I can understand why you might feel that way. But you don't know the whole story. When Queen Areya was still a girl, I was called to the palace to treat her. I was, thank God, able to cure her. I think she'll see me …"

The very idea—my Stoon Papa sweet-talking the Queen, calling in old favors! Maybe he could chat up the sun while he was at it. Ask it to please set a little later from now on.

I scoffed, "So what if she does? What can she do? Make Pol unchoose Dalil? I don't think so. After all, Dalil is an adult …"

My father wasn't listening. His own wheels were making too much noise in his head.

He stopped buttoning his coat. "Wait! I know! Why don't you come with me, son? We can state our case together."

My reply caught in my throat, snagging on opposing impulses.

Outright laughter.

Bitter tears.

His cause was hopeless. Still, I decided to do as he wished. After all, anything could happen to a Stoon crossing Gottika. We were safer when we traveled in pairs. My father needed me, whether he admitted it or not.

The Autumn Palace was on the east side of the city, in a grand park filled with deer and antelope. It was open to the public when the Royal Family wasn't in residence, but it was too far from the favela for most Stoons to ever visit, us having to be back by curfew and all. Like everything else good in our city, it was in theory open to everyone. In practice, it was reserved for Gottikans. As a result, I hated the place on principle.

When we arrived, tired and dusty, it was of course too late to request an audience. We didn't have enough money for a room at an inn, so my father and I spent the night huddled together with our backs against the stone footing of the iron fence. Luckily, no guards shooed us away. They were used to petitioners, I guess. Or maybe Queen Areya didn't want to be seen crushing citizens under the royal boot on her very doorstep.

When the sun rose, we went to a nearby hostel. It was advertising, "Hot Breakfast; Hot Water for Washing, 5G," so obviously we weren't the first people to spend a night against the fence. Maybe not even the first Stoons.

The gates opened precisely at 9:00 a.m. A guard showed us to a hut that housed a weapon detector. He forced us to remove all of our outerwear except for our *beretes*. Shivering in our underpants, we walked through the detector. The guards patted us down. When they were satisfied, they threw our clothes and shoes at us and pushed us out of the hut to get dressed in the open air.

"I bet they don't treat the Gottikans like this," I said, stepping into my pants.

But even as I griped, a Gottikan emerged from the hut clutching his bundle of clothing to his chest.

We sat on a hard bench in an otherwise bare room for *four hours* before an attendant in a velvet frock coat beckoned to us. "The Queen will see you now. Speak only once the Queen has spoken to you. Do not touch your face or hair in her presence. When she indicates your audience is over, do not turn your back on her. A courtier will take your elbow and guide you out of the chamber. Remember you are honored to be given this audience—do nothing to turn that honor to shame, or woe will be to you."

"You sure this is going to be okay?" I whispered to my father. My stomach was leaping and twisting like one of the antelope in the park. I doubted throwing up on the Queen would be a good way to maintain our family's honor—or to bring Dalil home.

"Don't worry, son. You'll see, these attendants put on far more airs than she does."

The Queen was a youngish woman, still blonde, still beautiful. But she was also regal. There was no mistaking she was royalty.

My father bowed low. "Good afternoon, Your Highness. I pray you remember me, your humble servant Judah Haleoni."

"Rob-Judah! Of course I remember you! You magicked away that disgusting *spot* on my arm when I was a girl. I was so grateful." She pointed her chin in my direction. "Who is this with you?"

My father introduced me. I made a clumsy attempt at a bow.

She acknowledged me with another lift of her chin. Then her expression subtly shifted. No longer was she the grateful girl. She was unmistakably The Queen.

"What can I do for you?"

My father explained how Dalil had been spirited away, in the dark of night, by Count Pol's men. How we couldn't know if it was Dalil's own choice to go. How her mother was upset.

As he related the tale, the Queen became more and more agitated. Her face flushed, her eyes flashed, her fingers tightened on the arms of her chair.

"And what do you think I can do about this? You know the Counts are responsible for their own districts."

"No one is safe, milady, if Pol is not reined in. Anyone

34

could be labeled a traitor. Even your own daughter. Think of the Princess. Think of Avivia …"

I was surprised by that. People never really talked about the Princess. And no one ever *saw* her. She was kept far, far away from the likes of us.

Queen Areya also seemed surprised, and not in a good way. She shrank back into her throne and fixed her gaze on the high windows. Her profile looked as if it was carved from marble.

"In truth, I have very little influence in matters like this. The Counts are their own law."

She fluttered her fingers in the air. Our interview was over.

Unseen hands whisked us out a small, plain door. We found ourselves in the deserted park. I smelled burning trash, its sour scent a portent of winter. With nothing to show for our efforts, we began the long trudge back to the Stews.

10

I heard what happened next fifth-hand. Dalil's mother, Luz, told it to my cousin Iris. Cousin Iris told it to her friend, Madelina, who is good friends with Mrs. Beanburg. Mrs. Beanburg told it to Beano, and Beano told it to me. So I can't vouch for the particulars, but I think the basics are accurate.

It was late. Naturally Luz was sleepless with worry over her missing daughter. So when she heard a noise outside, she leapt from her bed. Hoping.

There, at the bottom of their steep stairs, Dalil was unlacing her boots.

"Dalil? Is that you?" Luz cried, not sure if she was dreaming.

Dalil looked up at her. Cross, as usual. "Who else? You think an ax murderer would stop to take off his shoes?"

Luz has arthritis that makes it hard for her to walk—yet she tore down the stairs at full tilt and clutched her daughter to her breast.

"Oh merciful God! Thank heaven you are all right!" she supposedly said.

Dalil supposedly replied, "Relax, Ma! Let go of me already! Nobody kidnapped me, okay? I wanted to go! Have some fun for a change."

Luz could not believe her ears.

Here she was, practically *hysterical* with worry, and Dalil had been safe all along? But what was this business about *wanting* to go up to the castle? Had Dalil lost her mind?

Dalil reportedly *pushed* her mother off of her and *sashayed* into the kitchen, where she rooted around for something to eat.

She told her mother, "The Count picked me! Me! Of all the girls in Gottika! To be his wife! *Of course* I went. And it was great. There was always something good to eat, not like this … *slop.* I even had my own servants … Why would I want to come back to this dump?"

At this point in the story, Beano drew himself up and tossed his chin, perfectly imitating Dalil, acting as if *she* were the Princess Avivia.

When we'd both finally stopped laughing, Beano said, "In the end, Dalil insisted the only reason she left the castle was because 'some old biddy' showed up and 'kicked me out.'"

Was the "old biddy" the Queen? I wondered.

No. It couldn't have been.

Beano said, "Then Dalil announced that the engagement was still on, and she'd be going back to the castle as soon as possible. 'Just watch me!' she dared say to Luz. Like it was some kind of game! Unbelievable." Beano shook his head.

I wasn't surprised at all. Beano didn't know Dalil as well as I did. I had no doubt she'd be back at the castle as fast as her fancy little feet could carry her.

She was beautiful, very beautiful. No question about it—the prettiest girl in the Stews. But she was also spoiled, headstrong, vain, and unbelievably selfish. In other words, a right piece of work.

Sure, Dalil was my cousin. But who ever said you have to *like* your relatives?

11

When someone dies in a Stoon family, we hold a small prayer service at the graveside and then return to our homes for a week of mourning. We eat round buns, round fruits, and eggs, all served on round plates, to symbolize the circle of life. And we douse the candles in our traditional three-armed candelabras. We eat by the light of lanterns brought by our visitors, which they take away with them when they go.

It's true, Dalil was not actually dead. But as far as our family felt, she might as well have been. She had brought shame on us, on our entire community. She was dead to us.

What had she done? I'm sure you already guessed that she went back to the castle.

Count Pol called a half-day holiday. He ordered the entire district to assemble in Tian Square. As we stood in the hot sun, Count Pol emerged on the balcony, wearing his spooky metal mask and sporting a bright gold walking stick. Dalil was on his arm, dressed in a shimmery gown. She wore a sparkling tiara on her head, and a disgusting self-satisfied smile on her face.

A fanfare of trumpets rang out. The Count stepped forward. "I present you with the new Countess. She will now be known as the Highest of the High, Her Supreme Graciousness, La Jaconda!"

Even I couldn't believe it.

She had jumped in with both feet, and actually married the toad.

We held the mourning days at our house. Luz was incapable of doing anything but sobbing.

We smudged our foreheads with ashes and stashed our shoes away—we would walk barefoot for the rest of the week. We sat on low stools and covered all our mirrors with cloths.

My father led the prayers.

"Let us say now the Prayer for the Dead for the soul of our daughter Dalil Bat-Astra. May she rest in peace."

"Amen," we all replied. "Amen."

PART II

"The beginning of flight is falling."
—Babylonian Talmud, Sotah 44b

12

A gray pall settled over the Stews, and over my family in particular. No one wanted to mention Dalil's name around us, knowing we would flinch.

The return of the Troubles—intensified crackdowns on Stoons—made things even more miserable. There was no laughter in the streets, no familiar pleasantries exchanged as people conducted their transactions. Instead, everyone in the favela hurried through their business, heads down. "Just get it over with" became our motto.

Scuttle home, latch the shutters, hunker down.

A temporary relief only, because every morning dawned with the new fear: what would we discover when we unbolted our doors and windows?

Who by stone: which neighbor's windows had been smashed during the night?

Who'd been robbed?

Who'd fled?

The tally lengthened, day by day.

The grown-ups said, "This too shall pass."

They said tempers would cool and memories were short—the Gottikans would forget their anger. Or, more likely, another bright, shiny plaything would attract their attention and turn their eyes away from us.

"Trust us," they said. "All will be well."

We nearly-growns thought they were full of it. But what could we do? If they were helpless to act, we were even more so. We were like ghosts, gliding through the mist, neither alive nor dead. Just … waiting.

One day, during lunch at the café, I got up the nerve to ask my father why Stoons couldn't live outside the favela walls.

"Why the interest, all of a sudden?" he said, flipping the pages of his new technomancy journal. He scanned the fresh text avidly, like he'd been starving for words.

"It's not all of a sudden. I've been thinking about it for a while. But now, with the Troubles …"

My father kept turning pages and sipping his cocolat. "There will always be Troubles, Dany. Life is Trouble. Don't distress yourself."

"You're treating me like a baby. Just answer the question."

My father looked at me, *really* looked at me, for the first time in ages. His eyes darkened.

He beckoned the waiter over and whispered in his ear. A moment later, the waiter returned with two glasses of water.

My father took a deep draught, then tapped on his glass with his fingernail. The glass tinked sweetly.

"What do you say—is this glass half full or half empty?"

"Come on. I know what you're doing. The answer's both, okay?"

"Humor me. Half full or half empty?"

I crossed my arms over my chest. "Fine. It's half full."

He picked the glass up in his left hand. With one swift motion, he turned it over in the air.

The water stayed *in* the glass.

It shocked me, of course. Not because the laws of gravity appeared to have been suspended, but because he was doing this … this … *magic* where anyone could see him.

I quickly checked the tables around us. To my left, a young couple were quarreling—an intense *you-said-no-you-said* love spat. To our right, two bearded men were engrossed in a game of chess. Everywhere else, the hustle and bustle of waiters and clatter of cups continued.

Clearly no one besides me noticed the illegal magic in our midst. *Thank God*, I thought. *Thank God.*

Meanwhile, the fingers of my father's right hand were tracing graceful figures in the air. They made me think of two white butterflies in a *pas de deux*, swirling round and round each other, ever higher …

My father leaned toward me across the table.

"The perspective problem," he said, still holding the glass upside down. "It has less to do with the answers to your questions, and more with what questions you ask. In this case, the ultimate question is not whether the glass is half empty or half full. But rather, 'What's the stuff in the glass?'"

He quickly flipped the glass over again. And took another sip.

"Cold, refreshing water. Nothing better, is there?"

"Cut it out, Dad! Quit trying to distract me with word games and magic tricks. I asked you a serious question. Why don't you just answer it?"

He set the glass down on the table. A little harder than necessary. Some water sloshed over the rim, leaving a trail of glistening beads on the scarred wood. His tapered fingers drummed a tattoo on the tabletop, making the droplets shudder and shimmer.

He stood, fished in his pocket, and tossed a few coins on the table for the waiter.

"Come with me."

My father left the café with a determined stride, looking neither left nor right. I had to half walk, half run to keep up.

We wound our way through the Stews' narrow, cobbled streets until we came to a second square, dominated by the hulking presence of the Meeting House. The building bore the ancient emblem of our ancestors above its heavy doors. It had once been an important place of worship for us Stoons. But during the earlier Troubles, it had been allowed to fall into disrepair. I'd never been inside.

"You know our people come from a faraway place." He nodded toward the flame symbol on the crumbling wall high above our heads. "Even though we've been in Gottika for hundreds of years, they still think of us as foreigners."

"You know you still haven't answered my question."

"I'm getting to it."

We climbed the imposing flight of stairs. My father pushed his shoulder into the sagging door. It swung open silently, as if it had been oiled only a moment earlier.

The cavernous hall was dim and smelled of must, books, and dried-up lemons. Rows of seats stretched away from us in two decrepit regiments. An aisle between them led to a listing platform. A cabinet stood on it, and a lantern flickered above. The Eternal Light.

My father took my shoulders in both his hands. His breath was warm on my eyelids.

I tried to squirm free from his grasp but was pinned in place by his firm hands, his probing gaze, his utter intensity. All I could do was turn my face away.

"The rest of Gottika is safe for them. But for us, it's dangerous, because even after all these years, we're still different from them."

My jaw tightened. "We don't seem that different to me."

"That's because we're not. All people are the same inside. We are all made in the image of God. You know that."

His elusive, dancing words, the way they contradicted themselves, made me angrier than ever. I wanted my father to stop playing his mind games for once, and tell me the truth. *Were we different or weren't we?*

Before I could summon the words, he turned his back

on me. He took a few steps down the central aisle and raised his eyes to the Eternal Light. His long, lean figure was silhouetted by its rays. I couldn't tell if he was deciding what to say to me next or if he was praying.

Finally, he sighed. He rubbed his hands over his face and through his hair.

From across the gulf that separated us, he said, "We continue to live in the favela because, honestly, we 'Stoons' prefer it. It's … cozy. Isn't it?"

Now, *cozy* is not the word I'd use to describe the Stews.

I didn't think it was a word that my mom, staring at its looming walls, would use either.

On the way home, I realized my father was right on one count at least.

Half full, half empty—those things didn't matter.

The important question was: on which side of the gate was the bolt?

13

One Sunday morning my father bounded down the stairs, full of chipper good cheer.

"We haven't spent much time together lately, just you and me. Why don't we pack a picnic, go for a walk in the country? Maybe do a little fishing?"

So he wants to mend fences, does he? Fine, I thought. *Let him try.*

Truth was I hadn't slept well the night before—I found myself tossing and turning a lot these days—and I was too tired to argue with him. It was so much easier to go along with the plan. Besides, there wouldn't be much talking. The trout wouldn't bite unless we kept quiet. So I grunted my okay and choked down the rest of my breakfast. Gloppy porridge, same as always.

My father and I weren't the only ones passing through the monumental city gates—the sun was shining, and a rare breeze from the south had enticed plenty of other Stoons to escape the favela. Our numbers transformed the road into an endless ribbon of red. We walked amid the crowd for an hour. Then another hour amid the thinning ranks. At last we passed through an ancient wood. After that, we were alone.

Nothing now but birdsong and a dry heat rising from the roadbed. A hollow ache in my belly said lunchtime had come and gone. The blued distance wavered in the haze. We were nearing our habitual fishing spot. One we knew had mud trout in the shallows.

We forged our way through prickly shrubs to the riverbank, picking our way along it until we spotted the familiar landmark—an old knotted willow. It had been uprooted by a long-ago storm, and now leaned precariously out over the river. Its sheltering, greeny-yellow fronds stroked the water's surface like loving fingers.

We'd arrived.

I took a frayed blanket from my knapsack. Together, we spread it on the grass beside the willow's exposed roots.

My father flicked one rebellious corner into place. "It's good to get out of the city, isn't it?" He smoothed away the wrinkles. "Breathe some fresh air. Forget for a while about all the recent … events. It's been a long time since we went for an outing like this, eh?"

I couldn't even remember the last time, so I just nodded.

I yanked off my *berete*, threw myself down on the blanket. Shielding my eyes with the crook of my arm, I let our special place work its magic. Slowly but steadily, the knots in my shoulders unkinked.

My father tapped my hand. "Now, don't forget what I told you—keep a sharp eye out for bears."

I cracked one eyelid open. "Bears? Give me a break."

"I know it seems crazy. But they're a lot worse than they used to be. Because of Count Pol's little hobby."

At the mention of the Count, my fleeting sense of peace vanished. In its place was a cold lump of something. Congealed bear grease, maybe.

I rolled onto my stomach. Combing the damp grass with my fingers, I said, "I can't believe the Count's soldiers actually let bears loose so he could hunt them. How dumb can you be?" I yanked a twisted green clump from the earth and squeezed it in my fist.

"I know. It's incred—"

"And the Count is such a bad shot that most of the bears escaped!"

The clods of dirt swung back and forth on the bone-colored roots. *Tick-tock. Tick-tock.*

My father pried the tangled strands from my fingers. "Leave that alone. Those shoots are living things." He slipped a plum into my hand. "Here. Eat."

The plum was warm, and smelled sweet. I sighed and took a bite.

"Next thing you'll tell me doolves are real too," I said through a mouthful of fruit.

My father bit into his own plum.

I cocked an eyebrow. "So? Are they? Kids at school say they are. They say they are descendants of dogs abandoned during the Great Famine. They say they crossbred with wolves, and they're as smart as dogs but as fierce as wolves."

"Do they, now?" He was busy patting the limp grass back into the ground.

I knew in my heart my father wasn't listening anymore. But I kept talking, letting myself get more wound up with each sentence. Trying to make him pay attention, I suppose.

"Yes! They also say that the doolves still have feelings about humans, both good *and* bad. Like they remember how much they hated being kept as pets. But at the same time, they also remember how much they loved the people who cared for them. They say that doolves have evolved protothumbs. And that they have settlements more like human ones than wolv—"

"Fairy tales, Dany. It's all fairy tales."

"—*and* that they can *control* the *birds* and *termites*, getting them to weave mats and build dens!"

"You're getting carried away, Dany. You can't believe that nonsense."

I thrust my jaw out defiantly. "Does it make more sense to let man-eating bears escape?"

"No. I suppose not," my father said.

I took another decisive bite of my plum.

"Okay. So maybe all that crazy stuff is just that. Crazy. But doolves are real. In fact, Dad, I'm pretty sure I saw one."

I glanced at my dad, checking for a reaction. There was none.

I continued, "I was nine, maybe. I came across an abandoned dog in an alley. An ordinary enough puppy, I guess, except it had these weird red eyes. It didn't seem fierce at all. It was just a pup, in need of TLC and a good meal. I took care of it for a while, feeding it scraps and stuff. But it got too big. I had to send it away. The more I think about it now, the more convinced I am that it was actually a doolf."

My father tucked his feet under himself. "No … you're remembering wrong. It was a dog. Just an ordinary dog."

My temper rose. I was so sick of him treating me like a baby.

"You're lying, Dad! The way you *always* lie to me. You think I don't know? You think I'm stupid? You lie about the doolves, you lie about the Gottikans. And you lie about us. *Us*. We don't live in the Stews because we like it. Stoons live there because they *make* us. They *hate* us!

"No matter how we bow and scrape, we get nowhere. We're like … Pol's caged bears. Set free only so they can shoot at us." I clutched him by the shoulders. "There *must* be a reason why they hate us so much! It's time you told me why."

His narrow frame slumped beneath my fingers. "Why? Because they're afraid of us."

"Afraid? Yeah. Right."

"No. It's true. We once were a very powerful people. Dany, we weren't caged bears—we were lions! Rulers in our own land! We had knowledge that today we can only dream about … But most of our traditional wisdom was lost. During the Great Famine. We had to leave our land. And the digi-devices, the info-cloud, failed. In the end, we were only able to save the knowledge preserved in printed books. The mysticos at Lindisfarne, at Zefat, at Sedona, thank God they'd kept their knowledge alive in the old ways—on parchment and papyrus. All we have now, we owe to them.

"That knowledge, however, wasn't enough to sustain us. Without our own land, we became like this uprooted tree. Weak, fragile. Powerless."

"Now *that's* nonsense." I hurled my plum pit into the river. "Everyone has some power! But you're too chicken to use yours. You'd rather stick your head in the sand and hope everything will be rosy when you pull it out."

My father held both hands up in front of him. "Okay, Dany. You've got me. You're right, I've been … preoccupied. By simply trying to survive. Your mother …" He exhaled—one long, drawn-out, ragged breath. "I've barely got the strength to deal with the day-to-day, let alone to hope for something better. I stopped imagining the sky a long time ago … But what else can I do? They took my books, my tools. I've got nothing to fight with."

My nails carved half-moons into my palms. "Yes, you do!" I said, hurling my words at him like thunderbolts. "You always say we carry God within us because we have the power of speech. Isn't that what you've told me? So we do have power: we have words. *You* have words. Use them, for God's sake!"

"Dany! That's not fair! Haven't I spoken out? Didn't I try to rescue Dalil? The problem isn't that I don't try.

But sometimes, the tools at hand aren't what we need to complete the task. It's like trying to seal a hornet's nest with a dollop of jam. Nothing is easy, Dany. Even things that seem simple. You'll discover this for yourself when you are a grown-up."

I snorted. "Yeah, well, my thirteenth birthday's just around the corner."

"I know. Believe me, I know," he said, reaching for me.

"Let's see what magical difference that great day makes to my life."

He placed a hand on my hair. At his touch, my rage dissolved, leaving me limp.

"There's an old saying, Dany. Do you remember it? 'Even the angels have to live in the world the way it is, not how they'd like it to be.'"

"Stupid angels," I muttered.

14

Our shadows marched from one side of the blanket to the other as the sun continued its journey across the sky. Long past midday, when even birds resumed their chatter, my father and I were still fishing, silently, sitting with our backs to each other.

I imagined my father was nursing his wounded feelings, much as I nursed mine. I didn't know what I felt, exactly; I couldn't put my shapeless misery into words. I was restless, yes. And dissatisfied with everything and everyone, especially myself. But what to do about it? No idea. I only knew that I couldn't accept things as they were, not anymore.

Did my father read my mind? Or maybe he'd been having his own imaginary conversation with me in his head. Because he abruptly said, "I can promise you this, Dany: On your next birthday—when, according to the traditions of our people, you become a man—I will give you something special. A gift of great value. One I hope you'll use wisely." He looked deeply into my eyes. "I *know* you'll use it wisely."

He sighed. "I must be getting old—even my tongue feels heavy. What do you say we go for a swim?"

A good idea, at last.

"Last one in washes the supper dishes," I said.

We stripped and draped our clothes over a convenient shrub. Then we waded into the stream, feeling the soft silt slide away under our toes and the delicious, silken water gather us in.

It was pure bliss.

We swam, and we splashed each other, and we floated on our backs, watching the clouds shape-shift from swans to chicks and back again. I was thinking it was time to get dry, maybe even take a little nap under the trees, when a flash of light downriver caught my eye.

A pair of guards. Sunshine glinting off the barrel of their guns.

That wasn't good. Were they heading our way? If so, I'd prefer to be safely out of sight. No telling what a pair of guards could get up to out here in the countryside.

"Dad!" I called softly. "Look! Guards."

He raised his head and squinted in the direction of my finger. "I don't see anything. But then again, my eyes aren't what they used to be."

I looked again. The guards were gone.

Relief washed over me. Maybe they went the other way …

"Sorry, false alarm," I started to say, but then the guards burst from the brush. My insides went cold, then hot, then cold again as they strutted across the clearing.

"Looky, looky-loo … what have we here?" one of them said, kicking over the picnic basket.

The other poked at our clothing with his gun barrel. He scooped my *berete* onto its tip and raised it in the air. Letting the hat dangle limply from the end of his gun, he showed it to his buddy. Both guards smiled. The kind of smile that curled your hair.

Guard #1 pointed at me.

"You there! Out of the water. NOW!"

My father and I stepped out of the water and stood beside each other on the riverbank, shivering. We quickly threw on our clothes, and they stuck to our wet bodies. One of the soldiers passed a scanner over my father's wrist, reading the identification tag all adult Stoons had embedded in their skin.

"So, *Rob* Haleoni," he said with a sneer, "how come you and the kid weren't wearing your hats?"

The other soldier waved the two red hats in front of our noses.

"What? W-we were s-swimming!"

They laughed. The first one—the pug-nosed blond with the fan of zits across his cheeks—shoved my father.

"You think that's a good reason?"

The other one—the one with the squint—shoved my father back in the other direction.

"Don't you know the law? This is still Gottika Province, larv. HATS. ARE. MANDATORY. At. All. Times!"

Double shove.

Blondie caught me staring. He snapped his fingers at me.

"Let's see if a Stoon is any smarter than a dog. You there, larv. Sit, larv!"

"Wh-u-u-h?" I stammered.

Blondie took a menacing step toward me. "Do it! Now!"

My soul shrank to a cold, dark nub.

The guard with the squinty eye put a hand on Blondie's shoulder. "Ach, let it go, Rolf. They're not worth our time."

He thrust my hat roughly onto my head. "And make sure you wear these from now on, larvs. Next time you're caught without 'em, it'll be Noathic Prison. For both of you!"

He spat at our feet, and then they were gone.

15

My father placed tentative fingers on my arm.

"Son?"

I jerked away. "How could you? How could you just stand there and let them do that?"

"What did you expect me to do? They were *guards*."

"Why didn't you stand up to them? You were right— words *aren't* enough. Sometimes, you have to fight the way they do—with sticks and stones!"

I grabbed a branch lying in the grass and hurled it into the river.

"Dany! Dany! What's gotten into you?"

I turned my back on him. "I hate you! I hate you! I hate everybody! I hate this place! I hate everything about it!" I felt like I'd been taken over by a red-hot spirit of destruction.

My father reached for me, but I flung his fingers off my shoulder.

He said, "Oh no you don't, son. If you go running off in this state, you're bound to get yourself into trouble." He spun me around, threw his arms around me, and pinned my elbows between us.

I pounded on his breastbone. "Let me go!" I sobbed. "Leave me alone!"

"Shh … shh … it's all right. Everything's all right."

His grip on me loosened. I pushed myself out of the circle of his arms. My breaths came in huge, painful gulps. My mouth was dry and tasted like clay.

"Sorry, Papa. You know it's all just talk, right?" I shook my head, ashamed of my childish outburst. "That's all Stoons are: big talkers. Bark with no bite. When they kick us we promptly speak right up and say, 'Sorry for putting my butt in the way of your foot.' Sure, we're a people to be reckoned with. A proud people. People of the Useless Wagging Tongue. C'mon, let's go home. We've had enough fun for one day, don't you think?"

I turned my back on him and began walking. "Don't worry—I won't cause trouble," I said. I didn't even look to see if he was following me.

16

We tiptoed around each other for a few days. Overly polite. "Please pass the salt." "Of course, son. Would you mind handing me the butter?" "Certainly, Papa."

I thought this awkwardness would go away after a while. But it didn't.

Instead, odd things began happening. One morning, for example, while I was getting ready to leave for school, I heard weird thunks and crashes coming from upstairs.

The door to my father's study was closed. That meant "Do Not Enter!" I pushed the door open a crack anyway.

Inside, beakers and chalices containing liquids of all colors bubbled furiously. My father held a book up with one hand. With the other, he was pointing at a chair.

It was levitating in midair.

My father was doing magic. *Illegal* magic.

Over the next few nights, peeping through that same doorway, I observed my father as I'd never seen him before.

With his hair streaming out behind him, as if blown by an unseen wind.

With a mist of holy, mysterious, magic letters spilling from his mouth.

He uttered incantations so deep and dark it was as if they emerged from an underground cave. "Oh-ah-ee-ah!" The vowels vibrated and reverberated. "Ha-lai-lah ha zeh!" The syllables creaked and groaned.

I saw him with his robe glowing and his eyes flaring yellow. With candles dancing in a semicircle above his head, their flames casting eerie shadows on the walls, on his face.

When morning came, he kept falling asleep over his porridge.

I didn't know what to make of this new development. Unable to keep it to myself any longer, I confided what I'd seen to Ava and Beano while we were walking to school.

"Whoa …" Beano breathed.

Ava said, "That sounds … intense. You know we're here for you, right?" She squeezed my shoulder.

"Thanks. And back atcha, Ava."

Beano's brow creased. "What do you think he's up to? If he gets caught …"

"I don't know, Beans, but whatever he's doing, it's crazy. And I'm afraid it's going to kill him."

17

Another night, past midnight.

I was in that lovely half-doze when you aren't really in this world, but haven't quite left it either.

The front door slammed. I sat bolt upright, my heart hammering my ribs.

Who was entering? Or, even worse, who was leaving?

I strained my ears, listening for clues. No new noises downstairs.

I got to my knees and peered out the window. My father was striding down the street. His walking stick tinged faintly against the cobblestones.

I didn't like it. My father, out, on his own, well after curfew. And my father *never* used a cane—he walked perfectly well.

Who knew what he might do? And where exactly was he going?

I had to follow. I had to watch out for him. I tossed on some clothes and let myself out into the street.

Tailing him was easy. His *berete* caught the moonlight and shone like a beacon. The cane glimmered, too, flashing white with every step he took.

I wasn't surprised when he approached the favela walls. But I *was* surprised when he reached up and removed his hat.

His "light" went out. Allowing him to fade into the shadows.

Good call, Papa.

I had reservations about taking mine off. But I realized a hat was no protection for a Stoon out after curfew. If we got caught, we'd be in trouble. With or without our *beretes*.

I jammed my own "beacon" into my pocket.

My father slid deeper into the murk. His path clung to the favela wall and wound through a neglected park. Broken seesaws cast dragonish shadows on the bare dirt. One lopsided swing rocked idly in the breeze, releasing a metallic whine that made me shiver.

I knew this place—all the kids did. Concealed by a dead tree, a jagged crack squirmed its way up the wall. Ailanthus saplings, the "Tree of Heaven," had rooted themselves in it and against all odds clung to life. Here, getting over the wall was as easy as climbing a ladder; all you had to do was jam your toe in the crack and grab hold of the saplings to pull yourself up.

My father was over in an instant. I checked left and right, darted across the park, and heaved myself up and over too.

I followed him along the same route we'd taken that fateful day by the river. The city dropped away behind us. We were in the countryside.

With no streetlights to cast their weak protest, the night was blacker here. Only stars shimmered above us. Dogs—

or doolves—howled in the distance. The shadows looked alive. Owls hooted.

We entered the old wood. Night insects creeped and crawled and whispered all around us. They made the forest feel like a single, breathing organism. I wasn't sure where its boundaries ended and my own began.

Within the confines of the forest, I naturally remembered the old story about trees, and how they trap the souls of the dead in their embrace. Branches hold them fast until the souls are released by our prayers.

I looked up at the canopy. *Were there really poor, trapped souls up there?*

I willed my feet to step lightly, to not let a crackle of a twig reveal my presence. As I placed each tentative foot, one in front of the other, I said a prayer for those souls. I also said a prayer for my father. And yes, I prayed for myself too.

18

My father came to a stop at—surprise, surprise—that familiar bend of the river. I ducked behind a tree, safe within its shadows. My father, on the other hand, was starkly outlined by the rising moon. A full moon.

I still had no idea why he'd come here. Was he performing his own, private exorcism for what had happened to us?

Guilt ripped me apart. *Who was I to spy on him like this?* He was a grown man, with his own thoughts, his own purposes. He probably had a very, very good reason for coming out here in the middle of the night. Alone.

Yeah, right.

The riverbank was more mud than grass. His shoes squished. He prodded the ground with the walking stick, and I realized the cane was one that had belonged to my father's grandfather. It was tipped with a silver hand. Its index finger pointed heavenward. When you walked with it, the finger seemed to say, "Remember who is up there, m'boy." My father was using the tip of the silver finger to draw lines in the dirt—a complicated magical diagram. Circles and more circles. Connected by lines, snaking in every direction.

Next he marked the spaces between them. Filled them with letters, with signs, with I don't know what. Gradually the symbols merged, creating something singular.

A human figure.

What in God's name was my father doing?

He lifted the walking stick high. I heard his sharp intake of breath.

He chanted:

Oh Lord,
As you once set your mark upon us.
Set your mark upon this Earth.

Bring life to this clay,
Just as you once brought life into the clay of the first man.

And like that first man,
Let this man breathe the breath of life.

And, like the first man,
Like all men,
Let this Gol
Walk upon the Earth and
Do your almighty will.

He raised himself onto the tips of his toes three times. He roared, "I call upon you now, God, using your secret holy name!" A stream of fire burst from his mouth.

19

My father fell to his knees. His body thrashed this way and that, as if a demon inside him were struggling to free itself. And still the flames poured forth. I wanted to run to his side, but I held myself back—what could happen if I interrupted him? Would the flames consume him? Would they consume me?

There was no way of knowing. So I stayed put.

The fire sputtered and died. Oldtongue letters written in smoke flew from his mouth.

The first letter, a *yud*—shaped like a small, arched eyebrow ׳.

The second, a *hay*—like a safe, small house. ה

The third, a *vov*—a spear. ו

The alphabet of mist settled on the ground. It swirled over the drawing. Wherever the mist touched, the lines began to glow. The outline pulsed a burning white.

Steam rose. The boundaries deepened, as if an invisible knife were carving my father's lines down, down, down into the earth.

Inside the lines, the mud bubbled and boiled and swirled. The proverbial primordial ooze; a whirlpool of mud.

And then the earth thrust itself up, as if straining for the heavens.

I rubbed my eyes—was the mud coming together in a recognizable, three-dimensional shape? A *human* shape?

Yes. There—lying *on* the ground, at my father's feet. No longer a mere outline. But a fully realized person.

A man.

The fingers elongated and separated. The ears lifted away from the head and curved around like two delicate shells. The eyes. The nails. The lips … all took shape before me.

Little by little, the creature shook itself free from the earth.

20

The mud-man's head left a well of shadow behind, the way your own head does when it rises from the pillow.

It raised one hand, then the other. Flexed its fingers. Stared at them in wonder.

I was paralyzed with shock, with awe. And—let's be honest—with terror.

I didn't know what to think. I *couldn't* think. My father, before my very eyes, had used magic, to create a man. *Out of mud.*

The *thing* sat up—an amazingly lifelike sculpture. But its eyes were blank.

Papa brought one of his trembling fingers to the clay brow. With great care, he inscribed a series of letters upon it. First, the Oldtongue letter E. Then an M. Another E.

His voice rang out like a clarion. "Listen! Rob-Tanaka, the wisest of the ancient sages, said that all people have their characters described in words upon their bodies. Only the holiest among us can read them. As for you, a Gol, a man-made man—everyone can read *your* character.

The word I inscribe upon you is the Oldtongue word for 'Truth.'"

Plunging his finger into the damp clay once more, he added a T to the letters on the creature's forehead. Together, they spelled *Emet*.

Truth.

The Gol's irises contracted, leaving an empty space so deep and black there was room enough for all creation in it. The pupils lit up with a jagged flare, like lightning. The bolt took the shape of the Oldtongue letter B, the first letter of the first word in our Holy Book: Beginning. Answering flashes of lightning split the sky.

"Rise!" my father shouted.

The clay-man stretched himself up, up, up, until he towered over my father.

"Oh ... my ... God ..." I breathed.

21

My father handed some trousers to the Gol. The creature struggled to pull them on.

"Listen!" my father said. "I've given you life, and so I will be like a father to you. But I can't give you the ability to speak. Only God can bestow that blessing. So you can hear and understand all you're told, but your domain is silence.

"Yet you're far from powerless. You have eyes to see, and strength to act. With these gifts, you shall perform your appointed tasks:

You shall act only to protect our People.

You shall do no harm.

You shall remain obedient to me, and to my family.

Do you understand?"

The clay-man lowered his blazing eyes and nodded.

My father placed both hands on the creature's head. It's what one does when giving the traditional Stoon blessing to one's children.

"I will complete the process, then. I will share the secret holy name with you."

My father closed his eyes and breathed in deeply. Centering himself for prayer.

"May God bless you and keep you. May God's countenance shine upon you. May God grant you peace."

He placed his lips against the clay-man's and blew into his mouth.

The clay-man's body shuddered. Dried mud flaked off him, like a disintegrating shell. And what lay beneath! This was a clay-man no longer. He was a man—a living, breathing, flesh-and-blood man!

The giant turned toward me. Its eyes shone bright red. It lunged.

I tried to scramble away, but the boggy ground pulled me in, holding me fast. The earth was in league with him. With *it*.

The Gol growled. Huge, powerful fingers closed around my arm, my shoulder, my throat.

And there was darkness.

22

When I came to, I was flat on the ground. My father was clucking over me. The monster was sitting on a nearby tree stump.

I shrank back. "Papa! It was going to kill me!"

"No, he wasn't. He *can't* kill you. He can only protect our people. He's a Gol, a servant, created just for that purpose. He was protecting both you and me. Look!"

My father pointed toward the spot where I'd concealed myself. There, lying in the weeds, was a pile of … something. Matted fur.

"You were right, Dany. There *are* doolves. And they are much more vicious and clever than natural dogs or wolves. That one was stalking you. The Gol saw the doolf about to pounce. He saved your life."

"So doolves are real. Like I said," I mumbled. Trying to get my head around what I'd seen, what I'd heard. And not doing a very good job of it.

"There are many evils in this world, son. I didn't want you to know about them—yet. I wanted to shield you from pain a little longer … It's hard to remember you aren't a little boy anymore. I'm sorry I failed you, Dany."

I threw my arms around my father's neck. "You haven't failed me, Papa. Honest. It's me who's failed you."

The Gol sat. Waiting.

I couldn't help it—that … *thing* made my skin crawl. But it—he—had saved my life.

I let go of my father and, steeling myself, approached the Gol.

It was the right thing to do.

I took a deep breath and said, "Thank you."

Would he understand?

The Gol raised his eyes to mine. They were like the eyes of the doolf puppy I had once cared for. Soft. Vulnerable.

Yes. He understood me.

The sun was rising at our backs as the three of us headed home. The surrounding trees, gilded by the sun's rays, looked like candelabras. Some looked like *hamsas*, our people's traditional amulet. They symbolized the Hand of God, offering protection.

Was that what our Gol was? A hand of God?

We entered a glade where the morning mist still shrouded the trees in gray. They dripped with dew—or was it tears? I shivered, and thought again of the human souls bound up in their branches. Would they ever be free? Or were they, like the Gol, condemned to eternal silence?

PART III

"With a mighty hand
And an outstretched arm."
 —Psalm 136:12

PART III

23

Maybe it's best to imagine the next few days as Act 1 Scene 1 in a comedy of manners. We were the players, and the audience, and the play itself, making it up as we went. To this day I'm not sure who played the hero, and who the clown.

Imagine, for example, the look on my mother's face when we returned home. Even *she* couldn't be blind to this giant standing in her kitchen. He filled the room like a man-mountain, an Ararat, the way you do in a funhouse—the kind with the sloping ceilings and messed-up perspectives. But the clay giant was no illusion.

My mother fainted. Before she hit the floor, the Gol scooped her into his mighty arms and deposited her gently on the couch.

When she opened her eyes, my father was at her side. He offered a glass of water. She sipped it slowly, warily, eyeing the Gol.

My father, bubbling over with excitement and pride, told my mother what he'd done. He told her how the Gol was going to protect us from the Troubles and bring peace and joy back into our lives.

My mother spoke.

"Exactly how long is he going to be here, Judah? We can barely afford to feed ourselves."

Her voice sounded like a rusty hinge, but, oh! How beautiful it was to me! These were the first words that I'd heard her utter in, well, I can't say how long. Ages.

Did my father recognize how momentous this little speech was? That there was sound, where there'd been silence? Connection, where there'd been withdrawal?

He didn't seem to. He answered her as if conversation were a normal everyday thing for us.

"I told you already. He'll be here as long as we need him. We're facing danger from the Gottikans. We don't know what it is, or when it will come. So we wait. And our friend waits with us."

He took my mother's slender face between his hands. "The Gol was made to serve. So put him to work. I'm sure you can find something for him to do."

She glared at the Gol. He returned her gaze without emotion. He struck me as immovable. Not threatening. But not safe either.

No, he was definitely not safe.

My father believed he could control the Gol. I wanted to believe he could too. But even though I'd witnessed my father's powers in action, I doubted.

♦

My mother strove to think up tasks for the Gol.

She told him to fetch some water from the well. A few minutes later, I heard her cries, "Stop! Stop!"

I took the stairs three at a time, sure she was being harmed. But she was merely standing in a pool of water, a puzzled expression on her face.

She'd neglected to tell the Gol to bring only one bucket. He'd returned to the well, again and again, refilling the pail and pouring it into the sink until the sink overflowed.

The next task my mother assigned him was to peel potatoes. To avoid further catastrophe, she set *me* the task of watching over him.

Plunk! I threw my first peeled potato in the colander.

Plunk! I threw the second.

Plunk! When I threw the third, it occurred to me that we had handed this … *Gol* … a knife. So I watched him like I'd never watched anything before, alert to any sudden motion, any unexpected action.

But really, what could I have done if he had "evil intent"? He was the size of the house. He could hurt me without blinking an alphabet-filled eye. It didn't matter if he had a knife or not.

Plunk!

His potato landed in the colander.

Perfectly peeled.

24

What happened next? Nothing. The Gol didn't harm us in our beds. He didn't torch the favela. He didn't even eat us out of house and home.

Gradually, gradually, we got used to him. Beano and Ava did too. Once I got up the nerve to introduce them, that is.

Beano gave me a high five. "Not only does the whole favela have a bodyguard, but you finally have a sib too! What more could you want?"

Ava said, "And he's so cute! Like a big puppy! You know the kind I mean. With those giant paws and ears way too big for their puppy faces."

They were right. Living with the Gol *was* pretty amazing.

Even so, I never let my guard down, not entirely. But I did stop living with my heart in my throat.

One afternoon my father emerged from his study. He handed me a slate and chalk. "Teach him to read and write, won't you? So he can communicate with us better." He underscored his demand by shutting the door in my face.

Ha, I thought. *The Gol's not the only one who needs to learn how to communicate.*

I had no idea where to begin. No idea, even, how to approach him.

I stalled for a few days. Finally I decided to just take the Gol by the horns, so to speak.

I found him in the garden. Weeding the vegetable patch.

"Ah, er … Gol?" I said. "Papa wants me to teach you how to read and write. So when you finish what you're doing …"

He gave me that cool, level stare of his. Then he got to his feet and stood before me, waiting for directions.

I pointed to the shaded bench under the grape arbor. "We can sit there."

He folded himself onto the ground beside it.

"No! The bench," I started, but the Gol held up a hand. He pointed once to the bench, made a breaking motion with his fists, and then pointed to himself.

"Oh? It will break if you sit on it? You're too big?"

That long, level stare again.

I wrote out the letters Y, E, S, on the slate. "If you want to tell me 'yes,' you can write the word out here. See? These three letters spell out the word *yes*. Do you understand?"

Nod.

"Can you write them yourself?"

I handed the slate to the Gol. He fumbled with the chalk. Then he fit his fingers around it and managed to grip it as I had done. With total concentration, he copied the letters I had drawn. Miraculously, his own letters were perfect mirrors of my own.

"That's amazing!" I said. "I can't believe you did that on the first try!"

He held the chalk out to me and jerked his head. *More.*

He wanted to learn.

Well, well, well. As the old saying goes, *Knock me over with a phoenix feather.*

So I showed him his letters, and how to string them together into words.

One afternoon, my mother watched us. A smile played on her lips. "I remember teaching you how to read and write." She let her hand rest gently on my hair. "It seems like such a long time ago …"

A shiver ran through me. Yes—it *had* been an awfully long time. Since I'd been small. Since I'd seen my mother smile. Since I'd had a mother.

The Gol had brought her back to me. To us.

That was the greatest miracle of them all.

25

"You know, we still haven't named him," I said, pushing my chair back from the dinner table. "We can't keep calling him 'the Gol' forever."

The Gol watched me, passive but bright-eyed. He took a large bite of his apple.

"All right, then. What should we call him?" my father said.

"I've always liked the name Eli," my mom suggested.

"What about Elijah? In the Kumasha, Elijah was the herald of the messiah: *moshiach*, in Oldtongue. That would make sense for our own 'savior.' What did Rob-Tanaka write about Elijah? Let me think …"

My father closed his eyes, and that look came over him. The one that made him look like a prophet. The one that had made him a Rob.

He quoted the ancient text from memory: "Elijah searched for God in the chaos of the storm, but God wasn't there. He searched in the fire, but, still, God wasn't there. But then, in the very depths of silence, he heard a still, small voice …"

The quotation made perfect sense for our Gol. He was silent, after all.

My mother interrupted my father's recitation. "What about the name Mosheh, like the Mosheh who led the slaves from Eej and brought them to safety? I seem to remember Mosheh couldn't speak. That his older brother had to do the talking for him."

She looked at me pointedly and smiled.

"Hmmm … Moshiach, Mosheh—it works," my father said. "Our Gol will bring us to safety too—peace with Gottika. We can call him Moshe."

My father turned to the Gol. "So. Do you approve of the name?"

The Gol had almost finished his apple. It was nothing but core now. He popped the core itself into his mouth. Thoughtfully chewed some more.

He nodded.

My father chuckled.

"Eating the core—now that's something my grandfather would have called *moishe kepooyah*. 'He's a real *moishe kepooyah*, that one,' he'd say."

"What the heck does that mean?" I asked.

"I never really knew … Someone who's foolish or absentminded. Something like that. All mixed up."

An idea came to me. *Moshe … moishe …*

"Let's call him Moish, then! That okay with you?"

The Gol nodded again, then swallowed the core, seeds and all.

26

All was well, and all was well. Or was it?

With Moish at my side, I felt safer than ever before. More content, too, in ways I couldn't put into words.

But out in the real world, not much had changed.

The Gottikans still hated us.

Count Pol still spread lies and stirred up trouble.

And the Stoons worried.

One morning, I woke up earlier than usual. It was still dark.

The pallet Moish slept on—we had no bed large enough to hold him—was empty. The blankets were all a jumble.

Something was wrong.

I raced down the stairs and found Moish in the giant-sized armchair my father had specially crafted for him.

"What's happened? Where's Papa?"

He reached for the slate. Touched his chest. Touched me. Indicated the empty chair across from him.

I'd have to be patient if I wanted him to explain. I sat.

He took a deep breath, as if he were trying to compose his thoughts.

He put his hands to the side of his head, by his ear, and closed his eyes. Miming sleep.

Then he made a loud sniffing sound. And his eyes popped open.

"Something woke you. You smelled something?"

He nodded.

Moish mimed getting out of bed, tiptoeing his way down the stairs and out into the night. He placed his flattened hand like a shelf over his eyes.

My impatience got the better of me. "What? What did you see?"

He took the slate and quickly drew a picture. A wagon, being pushed and pulled down the road by two men.

"Were they Stoons?"

Moish shot me a look like I should know better. He aped coming up behind them—tiptoe, tiptoe. And then, looming over them.

Moish chased the two intruders down the street. He grabbed them by the scruffs of their necks, thumped their heads together, and knocked them out flat.

With one man in each hand, he brought them to his master, Rob-Judah.

I pictured Moish dropping the two unconscious men on the stoop like a cat delivering the gift of a mouse.

I had a harder time picturing what my father's face might have looked like when, still in his nightshirt and yawning, he opened the door to get the newspaper and found Moish sitting there, watching over his prisoners.

So that was that. The villains were foiled and Moish's story was done. All's well that ends well, they say.

I still had a nagging question. "What was in the wagon?"

He plucked at my shirt, my pants.

"Clothes?"

Yes. He mimed ripping cloth. Crumpling it.

"I don't get it."

Moish grabbed the slate, scribbled quickly, then handed it to me.

I read, "Bloodstains?"

Understanding dawned. "If a Gottikan's been reported missing ... and his clothes were discovered here ..."

Moish's faced drooped. His arms fell limply at his sides.

I stood up so abruptly my chair crashed to the floor. Outside, not far from our doorstep, stood the wagon. A knot of worried Elders clustered around it—my father, Raba-Caterina, Rob-Buda, Rob-Luria. No one enjoyed being woken before dawn. But this? To be faced with this threat, before the sun had even risen?

"Papa! Moish told me!"

My father looked up sharply. "Go back in the house, Dany. Everything's under control."

"Of course it isn't! *They* planned to frame us for the murder of a Gottikan! They were going to leave the evidence at our doorstep!" spat Rob-Buda.

Rob-Luria muttered, "Surprise, surprise ..."

"Do you think they really killed him? The guy whose clothes those are?" I asked.

"Dany, go inside. I already asked you once. Don't make me ask you again."

My father turned his back on me and continued talking with the other Elders. Their discussion sounded as if it were coming from the other side of a wall:

"We've got to get help …"

"Maybe the Queen?"

"She left for Praha. Last week."

"Count Rayn, then."

"Perhaps. He does tend to be fairer than most to the Stoons …"

I went back in the house. I made myself some toast but found I couldn't stomach eating it. I pushed it across the table to Moish. He pushed it back at me.

We sat like that, staring at each other, as the toast cooled between us.

There was nothing else to do but wait.

27

It wasn't long before the Elders came stomping in, wiping their feet, their voices loud. A plan had been made. They were going to go to Count Rayn and tell him the story before he had a chance to hear it from anyone else.

Moish would have to go with them.

They beckoned to Moish. He rose. I got to my feet too. I challenged my father with my eyes. *I'm not letting you go anywhere without me.*

My father nodded, one sharp, short nod. *Yes, you can come.*

The two thugs were bound and tied to the back of the wagon. Moish put the wagon's rope around his neck, and our grim parade set off.

Count Rayn ruled the Northern District of Gottika. Since our favela was not in his jurisdiction, there was nothing, technically, he could do to help us. The Elders, however, were hoping Count Rayn would lend us moral support. We knew Count Rayn had some sympathy for the Stoons. Or maybe, to be more accurate, little sympathy for Count Pol.

Count Rayn's palace was more manor house than castle.

No guards at the front. No massive gates. Just a polished mahogany door with a gleaming brass knocker.

To my utter surprise, Count Rayn opened his own door. *In his nightcap.*

Wow, was all I could think. *Things must really be different in the North End than in our part of town.*

Maybe the Elders were right, and Count Rayn *could* help us.

We'd need more than superstitions and luck, though, to survive this.

Count Rayn invited us in. Asked us to wait. My father agreed but said Moish would remain outside to guard the prisoners.

When the Count returned, freshly shaved and smelling of cologne, my father explained the strange events of the previous night. He described Moish as "my nephew from the country, awakened by a noise," and finished his account with "… so we thought we'd come to you before anything worse happened."

"Yes, yes. That was very wise." The Count called to a steward. "Tell the three men outside to come in. Keep a close eye on them."

Moish led the two thugs in, keeping a firm grasp on their ropes.

I wanted to laugh. Moish looked so … regal. The two Gottikans? Well, they looked guilty as all get-out. Shamefaced, stupid. They kept bumping into each other as they walked, and arguing over whose fault it was.

Count Rayn beckoned first to the man on the left. "So. What do you have to say for yourself?"

Timidly, the man stepped forward and told his tale. A garbled, transparent mixture of nonsense and self-serving lies.

The second man told a similar tale. *Similar*, mind you. But not the same. He couldn't get his story straight *even when he'd just heard it told.*

The look of disgust that crossed Count Rayn's face spoke volumes.

Wearily he said to his steward, "Very well. Call the Militia. Have them take these … bits of slime to the North City jail. And the evidence … bring it to Count Pol's castle. It probably belongs to someone from his district. Let him get to the bottom of this."

On our trip home, we were all exhausted. Rob-Buda seemed almost giddy with it. He clapped my father heartily on the back. "You did well tonight, my friend."

My father glanced back at Moish, who was scanning both sides of the road for danger.

"Don't thank me. Thank the Gol," he said.

PART IV

"Words in the heart are not words."
—Babylonian Talmud, Kiddushin 49b

To His Illustriousness
Count Pol
Peer of the Realm of Aloise
Liege of King Lo and Sworn Protector of his Queen,
Areya the Commendable
Administrator of the South District in the
Capital City of Gottika
and
Honored Compatriot—
Attached herewith are the pertinent documents
regarding Stoon Incident 32-12-47962. The evidence
contained in the report is undeniable—the two men
now in custody have completely **cleared the Stoon
community from all wrongdoing** in this matter.
I have no doubt that these *thugs* were not acting on
their own, but were rather *agents provocateurs* acting
on behalf of persons or organizations yet unidentified
with the intention to damage the good name of the
Stoon community.

Since this crime occurred in your jurisdiction, I
will arrange for the transfer of the perpetrators to
your custody forthwith. I trust you will thoroughly

investigate this matter and discover the truth of who is behind this low and despicable crime.

Please advise as soon as you determine the truth.

Yours in brotherhood, etc. etc.,
Count Rayn

On Order of His Royal Highness King Lo
To administer the North District of the
Capital City of Gottika

28

The next day, Count Pol declared a citywide "Day of Investigation." There'd be no work. Instead, the whole town was invited to see the clothes displayed at the castle. Was it a farce? A nod and a wink to say, *What a good joke we played on those Stoons*? Not necessarily. If the bloodstains were real … maybe someone would recognize the clothes and shout, "My son! My missing son!"

The gravity of the situation seemed lost on many. *Tra la, tra la*, off everyone skipped to enjoy the show.

Beano and I waited two hours in the line. Then we entered a dark, dank chamber, lit only by flickering torches.

We shuffled closer. The lady in front of us sighed and fanned herself with a faded flowered kerchief. To no one in particular, she said, "It takes the starch out of ya. Such a sad thing … Surely someone will recognize …"

A murmur of agreement passed through the crowd.

"Can you see?" Beano asked.

"Not really …" I rose up on my toes and craned my neck to get a better view.

The items for inspection were arranged upon the bier with ceremonial precision:

A pair of scuffed shoes, the laces gaping.

Slim gray trousers, pressed flat.

A green and yellow striped shirt with a jagged hole torn in the front. The edges of the tear were rusty black, and curled up like the lips of a wild animal.

A watch with a smashed face.

I couldn't take my eyes off the shoes, with their laceless eyelets and shadowed hollows.

They were exactly like mine.

Someone in the crowd exclaimed, "Saints preserve us!" I turned instinctively to the voice but didn't see the speaker; instead I noticed, with a shock, my cousin Dalil standing at the far end of the bier.

Dressed in a rich gown of gray watered silk and clutching a lace handkerchief in her left hand, she dabbed delicately at her eyes, even though they were perfectly dry. Her face was pale, but composed, and as breathtakingly beautiful as always.

"I can't believe it! Dalil is here!" I hissed. "That … that …"

Beano gripped my elbow. "Keep your head, Dany. She's got nothing to do with us. You hear me?"

I shook his hand off. *Yes, I should ignore her. But how could I?* My heartbeat echoed in my ears, and my head spun with dark, angry thoughts.

How could she do it, play at being the hostess of this grotesque show? Didn't she know this crime was causing us all so much pain? Didn't she care?

The line shuffled us closer and closer to Dalil.

"Thank you for coming. Yes, it is strange, and awful," she said, over and over again. Her voice was as brilliant and clear as cut glass.

What would I do when I reached her? What would I say? What would she say? I hadn't a clue.

The line split, and, urged on by the press of people, I found myself jammed against the velvet rope that encircled the bier. The flickering candle transformed the pathetic pile of clothes into something else entirely. Something ominous.

We came to the end of the rope. Dalil was so near I could smell her perfume.

Attar of roses.

Our eyes met. I don't know what mine revealed, but hers gave away nothing. Not a hint of recognition. I knew she was faking. She most certainly knew me. And I knew her.

Or did I?

Was the girl I once called cousin still in there, beneath that polished mask? And did she feel as sickened by this spectacle as I did?

How could she not?

Dalil took my hand in hers. With practiced politeness, the "Countess Jaconda" thanked me for coming. Her cool fingers squeezed mine.

Her eyes flicked to the next person in line. Barely a second had passed, but someone else had already taken my place.

They were welcome to it. The scent of roses had always made me gag.

"Don't look now," Beano said, "but there's the Count."

Sure enough, the telltale gleam of a gold walking stick flashed in the shadows.

I knew why Dalil was there. She was a glittering jewel to distract and provoke the crowd.

But why would the Count hang around this cesspit?

He was watching us. To see if anyone reacted when they saw that gear.

And if they did?

My bet was they'd never find their way to the exit.

29

A month passed. Then another. No one came forward to identify the clothing. No one came forward to say their friend or relative was missing, either. Tensions didn't fade. If anything, the atmosphere in Gottika grew more strained. I hadn't realized it was possible.

One day I went downtown with Beano to deliver a carton of apricot preserves. Not many of the Gottikans still gave his mother their business, so her remaining clients were more important than ever.

"Thanks for coming with me," Beano said. "I'd never make this trip now if I didn't have to. Having you guys with me makes all the difference." He tipped his head to Moish, who trailed us at a discreet distance.

Both sides of the street were packed with Gottikans. As we passed, they stopped doing whatever they were doing and stared. Forget about trying to be inconspicuous: we might as well have worn outfits that flashed "Stoon" in neon letters across the back.

"Did I tell you the last time I made a delivery—without you and Moish—I was so scared?"

"Yeah, you told me."

"This is better. Even if the way they look at us makes me feel like I have three heads."

"Hey, didn't anyone mention it to you before? You do, Beans. You do. And the one in the middle? It's the ugliest."

Grinning like a goof, he punched me in the shoulder.

"So how's … Ava?" I asked, wincing at the off note I detected in my voice. *Jealousy.*

I had no right to be jealous. Moish was *almost* a sib …

But not quite. Ava was the real deal.

"She's good. But I worry about her. She goes out on her own all the time. I freak until she gets back. Like right now I'm hoping she'll be at home when we get there. She took off somewhere this morning, didn't say where she was going."

"Stop being such a worrywart. She's fine."

He gave me a withering look. "You don't know that. And c'mon—be honest —you'd have to be crazy not to be worried these days. Not everybody has a 'cousin' to watch over them 24-7."

I smiled, picturing Moish standing near the city gates like he did every evening, arms folded across his massive chest, his face a steady mask.

"Yes, they do. We all do."

30

No defense is perfect. Not even a Gol.

This time, their plan succeeded.

Here's what happened:

In the wee hours of the night, two men came over the wall. Moish saw them. He gave chase.

So he was no longer at his post when the third man vaulted over and slithered his way into the Stews.

Nor was Moish at our house when that slimedog slunk into our yard through the back gate.

There were no watching eyes to see him bury the bloody knife, wrapped loosely in a piece of fine cloth, behind the patch of yellowing chrysanthemums.

The Militia kicked down our door at dawn and dragged my father from bed. They laughed and mocked him. "Kick all you like, little Stoon, you won't wriggle off Count Pol's hook this time!"

I started to go to him, but my mother stopped me with a sharp shake of her head. *Keep out of sight*, it said. *Keep quiet.*

I shrank back behind my bedroom door, split by competing impulses: Obedience. Fear. Fury.

Meanwhile, sniffer dogs explored our house. One scratched at the back door. When the dog made a beeline for the 'mums, my father's fate was sealed. He was taken to the castle dungeons.

The reason? A Gottikan had gone missing. Abducted, it was said.

The knife that was found in our yard was "proof" of my father's involvement.

I don't think the Gottikans really believed my father was guilty. But what did it matter, as long as a Stoon was made to pay?

The price would be high, because this missing Gottikan was not a nameless, faceless nobody. She was from a prominent family.

The *most* prominent.

Her name was Avivia.

She was the Princess.

31

They said the Queen was beside herself with grief.

They said the King would not rest until the Princess was recovered, safe and sound.

They said this time there would be no mercy for the Stoons.

But we Stoons were not as alone, as cut off, as they thought.

We still had Moish.

And although we didn't know it then, we had another ally too.

32

With my father in jail, my mother collapsed again into silence. The Elders looked as horrified and helpless as she did.

It was Moish I turned to. I trusted he'd figure out a way to get into the dungeons and rescue my father. The determined look on his face—determined as well as fierce and intelligent—was something to behold. It actually scared me. I'd hate to be on the receiving end of all that concentrated, purposeful power.

Moish and I hid in the bushes, safely beyond the line of guards that surrounded the castle. I couldn't see how Moish could bypass them; he wasn't exactly inconspicuous. How would he get into the castle, find the dungeons, and rescue my father? He was powerful, all right, but he was still flesh and blood.

Nevertheless, he was the only hope we had.

Moish sensed my anxiety. He placed one of his huge hands on my chest, right over my heart. *Stay calm,* he was saying.

He put a finger to his lips. *Stay quiet.*

He pointed to the sun, and then lowered his hand.
Wait until night falls.

♦

The sun set.

Moish ordered me to stay put while he scouted. He slipped between bushes like a shadow. He seemed part of the landscape. And really, when you think about it, wasn't he? He was made of earth, of rain, of roots. His human form was the magical part, not his talent for melting into the mist.

For me, though, it was the same old story—sit and wait. I gnawed on my fingernails, watching for Moish's return.

The underbrush rustled. *Was Moish back already?* I checked left and right. *No.*

The noise got louder. It was coming closer.

I couldn't just sit there! I had to see what it was.

Heart pounding, knees quivering, I crept toward it.

33

My head swam with relief.

It was my father!

"Thank God you're safe!" I hugged him tighter than I had in years.

"*Wo-ho!* Let me breathe, son!" He held me at arm's length and studied my face. "My beautiful, wonderful child. What a miracle to find you here. Safe! Is your mother …?"

"She's fine," I said. Or she would be, now that my father was free. I hoped so, anyway. I pulled my father to me again and buried my face in his shoulder. His coat smelled of sweat, and smoke, and iron. Of fear.

"Dad," I murmured. The single syllable was delicious on my tongue.

Something rustled behind him.

And a voice: "Oh. It's you."

Dalil!

"Quit the love-fest, fellas, till we're out of danger," she said crossly.

I gaped at her. "What are *you* doing here? How did you get here?"

"Secret passage. Now, do you mind? Move it, petunia." Dalil prodded the small of my back. "We don't exactly have time for a chit-chat."

She set off at a jog.

Moish was suddenly *there*, blocking her path. His eyes were red, red beacons of fury. He reached for her.

Dalil's eyes went wide. Her mouth opened and closed, gasping in vain for breath.

"No! You mustn't harm her!" my father said.

Moish dropped Dalil, but he still loomed over her, glaring, his eyes that dangerous red. A growl emerged from deep in his chest. Dalil shied away.

My father took my cousin in his arms. He stroked her hair and cooed gentle words of comfort. She was crying now, pale and small, against his shoulder.

"You must not harm her," my father repeated, his eyes fixed on Moish's. "You *cannot* harm her. She's a Stoon, Moish. She's one of us."

34

We ran through back streets, waiting for Moish's beckoning finger to indicate the coast was clear.

We passed through quiet closes where only rats moved, and crept across gardens where families ate supper behind plate-glass windows. Hearts pounding, breath coming in ragged bursts, leg muscles afire, we made our way to the outskirts of the city and beyond it.

To the countryside, and the safety of the woods.

To the familiar riverbank, where our savior, our Gol, had been forged.

We slumped against the fallen tree, regaining our strength.

Questions tumbled in my mind, squabbling for the right to be asked first.

"We owe Dalil an unpayable debt of thanks," my father said.

I glared at her. "I thought *Dalil* was dead."

"I thought so too," she said. "I was wrong."

"Oh yeah? So what changed your mind, *Jaconda*?"

"Something that happened on that day I saw you. Do you remember that day?"

"Of course. The 'Day of Investigation.' You were standing beside the bier. You were thanking people for coming."

Dalil's eyes slid away from me. "Yes."

So she was embarrassed. *Good.* I still wasn't gonna let her off the hook.

"You didn't even acknowledge me."

"You didn't exactly say, 'Hi, cuz,' either," she snapped.

But then she blinked and shook out her hair, like she was shrugging off a bad memory. "I'm sorry. That was uncalled for."

I snorted. "No joke."

"Dany," my father said. "Stop baiting Dalil. Let her tell her story."

"Fine." I swept my arm toward the bare ground. "The floor is yours, *Dalil.* Or whatever you're calling yourself today."

35

Dalil settled herself more comfortably against the fallen tree and began her tale. She still loved an audience.

"I was there, in that dismal chamber. All day. Not that I wanted to be. But the Count had commanded it. And when Count Pol commands something, you'd better do it. He told me I was his eyes and ears. He told me to watch for any glimmer of recognition—shock, horror, despair, whatever—when someone looked at the clothing.

"Of course I'd have told him if I'd noticed any. That was the whole point, wasn't it? To find out who the stuff belonged to?

"So many people filed past me. Tsk-tsking, tut-tutting. But no one said a word. No one. That was impossible! How could someone go missing and no one come forward?"

"So you don't think the torn clothes were faked?" I asked.

Dalil snorted. "That's not Pol's style. He loves plucking up random people and locking them away. Those clothes had to belong to somebody. About ten million hours in, when still no one had stepped up, the light went on in my head. Someone *did* know whose clothes those were. Pol himself."

I must have made a face, because Dalil directed her next words to me.

"Whatever else you may think of me, Dany, I'm not stupid. Or completely heartless. I knew Pol liked to amuse himself by stirring the propaganda pot, and that he wasn't above adding his own spice to it. I knew that was one of the reasons he married me. But I closed my eyes to all that. Went 'la-la-la' and pretended I didn't know." She stared at her cuticles. Took a deep breath. "The truth is, once you know something, you can't un-know it. No matter how hard you try, Truth will yank your fingers from your ears and pry your eyelids open. She'll demand you look her straight in the face.

"It was clear as day that Pol knew who the missing guy was. And who'd abducted him. Because Pol was the one who'd ordered his kidnapping."

I couldn't suppress a bitter laugh. "I get it. You thought you needed a little insurance to protect yourself from your new hubby. How very selfless of you. How noble."

"I never claimed to be noble, Dany. And you're right. I did want a little insurance. I have a great deal of respect for my own skin."

"That makes one of us."

"Dany …" my father warned.

"Sorry," I said. "Go on, *Jaconda.*"

121

She fluttered her hand and bowed her head in mock thanks.

"That evening when Pol had to 'attend to some business,' I followed him. Tracked him like a doolf stalking dinner. He didn't head to the dungeons, like I'd expected. Instead, he went to the kitchen gardens. A pair of servants were kneeling in the dirt there, harvesting cabbages.

"Pol said, 'You! You there! And you, woman! Come with me. I have a job for you.'

"The servants leapt to their feet as if they'd been shocked by a cattle prod. Two of their cabbages rolled away. Pol led the servants along a long, dark passageway. The walls dripped. The air stank. The chill crept down your neck like it was warning you: *Don't go there.*

"Those poor servants. At the top of a steep stair, they hesitated. Pol snarled, 'What are you waiting for, dunces?' The man apologized, offered his wife his hand, and helped her down the stairs.

"I covered my face with my veil before I peeped down— better safe than sorry, eh? There was a narrow stone path at the bottom, lit only by a pair of torches on the wall. They cast this eerie, greenish light on the oily water and the slimy stones.

"What's that old saying? 'The grander the house, the deeper the cesspit'? Well, it's true. Pol had brought his servants down to the sewers.

"But—why? Before I could figure it out, Pol pushed the two of them into the shadows. The man yelped.

The woman screamed. Pol reached out and a metal door clanged shut.

"'Don't leave us here!' the woman cried out.

"Pol pulled a long black key from under his cloak. He twisted it in the lock. The cold scrape of it was the most terrible thing I'd ever heard.

"He touched his fingertips to his lips, kissed them, and fluttered them in the air. 'Nighty night, sleep tight,' he said. Then *plunk, plunk*, he tossed the key into that dark water.

"I should have turned around then and run. Run without stopping, out of the castle, out of Gottika, out of the country altogether. But my legs wouldn't move.

"Pol closed his eyes and leaned back in relief against the wall, even as the wails of the servants echoed around him.

"He started, and he peered up the stairs. I thought maybe he'd heard me. I pressed myself into the wall, praying he wouldn't see me. He seemed satisfied he was alone. He knelt and peered into the water—I don't know why. Maybe to make sure the key had disappeared forever. Before he rose, I backed away and fled down the corridor."

36

"It must have been horrible," my father said.

"Witnessing that ... that *evil*, broke me." Dalil dragged her sleeve across her eyes. "The moment Pol locked that door, my fantasy world melted to nothing. I could no longer deny that my 'One True Love' was a tyrant. Or that, in my heart, I also knew whose clothes they were."

My father and I stared at her. Dalil thrust out her jaw.

"Yes. I knew. They belonged to the son of those two servants. Yeah, I knew them too. One day in the garden, they'd been showing him off, their beloved child, to the other servants. Back from University in Praha, he was! Their pride and joy.

"They'd made such a pretty sight, under the flowering almond. Beaming Mother and Father in their tidy work uniforms, Handsome Son in his crisp school clothes: a sharp green and yellow shirt and natty gray trousers. He handed around a watch he had won as a prize in Philosophy ... I saw how they loved each other. I could even feel a little piece of that joy I recognized on their faces. I'd never understood it before …

"That whole family, locked away in the dungeons—I'm sure that's where the son is too. His parents probably had no idea he wasn't safely away at his University.

"The world is now a darker place than ever, because Pol loves hate more than he loves even himself.

"The morning after the sewers, I smiled sweetly at Pol over breakfast and told him he was magnificent. But in my heart I cried out, *My God, what have I done?*"

When Dalil had composed herself, my father asked, "How did you do it? Get me out of the dungeons?"

Dalil shrugged. "It was easy enough. It just took a bit of time.

"First, I needed a mold. So I melted a candle and let the wax drip into one of the drawers in my jewelry box—without the jewels in it, of course. Then I swiped a key from a sleeping guard. It only took a second to press the key into the wax; the fool never even knew it was gone. Didn't stop snoring the whole time.

"Then I got busy melting down some gold. Luckily, Pol has given me bucketloads. I poured the metal into the wax mold, waited for it to cool, and *abracadabra!* Dungeon key, at your service. You know the rest, Uncle."

"He knows, but I don't," I said. "How did you get my dad out of the castle?"

"All it really took, in the end, was patience. The key worked. I used some, ahem, magic, to untie his bonds—"

"You know magic?" I said, shocked. Practicing magic had been illegal for so long … and, well, girls didn't usually …

This time it was Dalil who raised her eyebrow at me. "Are you really so clueless? For God's sake, our whole family's been alchemists for twenty generations. You'd have to be living in la-la land to avoid picking up a trick or two along the way."

I shrank under her scorn. But then I felt Moish's hand on my shoulder.

I looked up and saw the letters on his forehead. EMET— the Oldtongue word for truth.

His message was as clear as if he'd delivered it out loud: Dalil was using her biting words as a smokescreen. They were nothing but false bravado.

When I returned my gaze to Dalil, she no longer seemed so sure of herself. She just looked scared.

Moish taught me two things that day. One, that words only gain power over you if you give it to them. And two, that you must sometimes look behind words, to what lies beneath them, to discover the truth.

37

My father took up Dalil's tale.

"Once my hands were untied, Dalil led me through a warren of underground passages. We ended up at a kind of boat landing, where a rowboat was tied. It carried us under the castle, and far beyond the walls. Eventually the water petered out. The boat scraped bottom. We got out and walked. The air was musty—Dalil's torch went out. From then on, we had to feel our way blindly.

"Gradually the path angled upward. The air changed. The ceiling dropped until we had to crawl on our hands and knees. Dirt surrounded us on all sides now—above us, below us. I began to wonder if Dalil had led us to a dead end … to our tombs.

"A glimmer of light appeared. It was the night sky, still holding a bit of twilight. We scrambled toward it and emerged from the earth. What a miracle it was that it was you, Dany, who was waiting for us there, and not the Militia!"

"Right. That was then. This is now," Dalil said, adjusting her shawl. "We're not safe yet. We should get beyond the borders of Gottika before morning." She rose to her feet. "Rest time over—let's move."

Moish pointed to himself and shook his head.

Then he pointed to me, and back toward the city.

"You want us to go back? To the city?"

He touched his heart, then touched mine.

Our mother, he was saying.

"Mom isn't safe," I said dully. "You want us to go back and get her?"

Moish nodded.

"Moish is right," my father said, coming to my side. "Once they realize I'm gone, they'll go after her. If they haven't already. You know the way. You can slip in and out of the favela unseen. We'll wait here for you."

I wanted my mom to be safe, but I didn't relish the idea of the long trip back to town, even with Moish. With Pol's Militia on the lookout for us. With wild doolves on the loose, and bears …

At the same time, we'd be leaving my father without protection.

I tried to delay the inevitable. "Why didn't we get her before we came all the way out here?"

Dalil smirked. A smirk that said: *You always* were *a wimp.*

I straightened my shoulders. *No way would I let Dalil make me feel small and insignificant ever again!*

"I can manage on my own. Moish will stay with you. To keep you safe. I'll go as quickly as I can," I said, my voice firm. "I'll bring supplies too. Food, tarps. You can count on me."

I expected my father to argue with me. Instead he said, "I know. Go safely and return to us safely, my child," and kissed me on both cheeks.

38

I reached our house a little before midnight.

My mother was sitting in the kitchen, staring at a plate of uneaten dumplings: eyes unfocused, hands empty. How would I get her to the river if her crying sickness had returned?

But when I called out, "Mom! Mom!" she flew to the back door and opened it for me. Crushed me in her arms and said, "Tell me—is there any news? Is he still—alive?"

I untangled myself from her and said, "Yes, yes. He's okay. You'll never believe it—Dalil helped him get out of the prison! Yes. I know! *Dalil!* He's at the river. Where we used to picnic. He sent me to get you. And we have to hurry."

My mother grabbed two knapsacks and filled them with fruit, with crackers, with cheese. She sent me scurrying through the house to collect warm clothes, blankets, rain gear. Insect repellent.

She locked the front door, then shoved the living room sofa up against it. When she saw me gawping, she laughed.

"No reason to make their next door-kick easy. I hope they break a toe."

We trudged side by side along the route. Anxiety rolled off her. She wouldn't relax until she saw my father with her own eyes and could reassure herself that he really was all right.

What would we have done if my father hadn't been rescued? If he had, in fact—

There'd be just Mom and me. On our own.

Which begged the question. The eternal Stoon question.

"Mom?" I asked. "Why are almost all of us kids onlies?"

My mother rounded on me. "What's the matter with you? Your father is in serious trouble and all you can think about is having a sib?"

"Oh, come on, Mom. Of course I'm worrying about Papa. That's why I'm asking. You owe it to me to tell me. To tell me the truth."

My mother sighed, shifted the knapsack on her shoulders.

"Fine. You might as well know. You're practically thirteen anyway. But I have to warn you: It's a long story."

"It's a long walk."

She sighed again.

"For the answer to your question," she began, "we have to go right back to the beginning, to the time of the Great Famine …"

39

"None of us alive today can imagine how horrible the famine was. They say it struck our homeland especially hard. Our ancestors were forced to leave to survive. We scattered, like seeds on the wind.

"Some of the wanderers, of course, found themselves in Gottika. The king of the time was named Alexander. He welcomed them. He knew of our people's skills with magic and healing. One of our Elders even became the King's honored advisor.

"Our people prospered here. Our numbers grew. Then King Alexander died. His successors forgot about him. They also forgot our ancestor.

"A new king came to Gottika. His name was Ahas. He saw how many of us there were. He said to himself, 'What if these people rise against me? They could take my city and conquer my kingdom.'

"He decided to put restrictions on us. No weapons, for example."

"The hats," I offered.

"Yes, the hats. You know most of the prohibitions already. But not all. Ahas's worst law was that no Stoon could have more than one child. Those who defied the ban 'disappeared.'"

My hand rose to my throat. "What happened to them?"

"No one knew. One day, they were there. The next, *gone*. Rumor had it that they were sent to secret work camps in the mining fields. A few returned. Sent as a warning to others in the favela. They wouldn't talk about what happened."

"What about the kids? What happened to them?"

My mother's reply was sharp. "The forbidden children? Or the ones that had been left behind?"

"Both, I guess," I mumbled.

Her eyes took on a faraway look. "Childless Gottikans could adopt them. Aristocrats, mostly. But if a peasant couple needed more hands to work the farm, they could request a child and raise it as their own. The adopted ones never even knew they were Stoons.

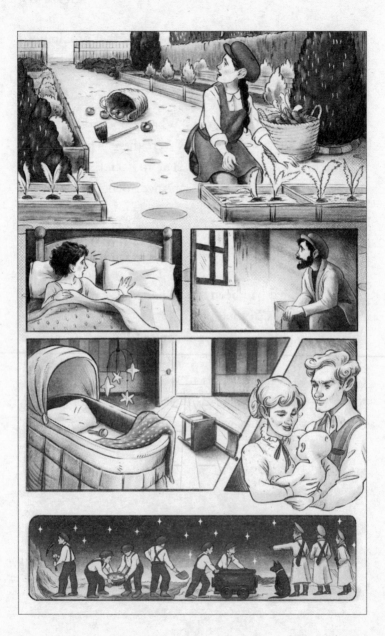

"The toll it took on us ... Can you imagine walking through the streets of Gottika, and seeing your son—and you *know* he's yours, the child's the spitting image of your aunt or husband or brother—in another woman's arms? Or you pass a girl who's a perfect duplicate of your sister—the one who disappeared eight years earlier?"

"How many were there?" I asked in a whisper.

"Thousands. Thousands."

"So it's true, then. What Papa says. That we and the Gottikans really are more alike than different. After all, lots of them *are* Stoons."

My mother reached out and took my hand in hers.

"Yes. But *all* people are more alike than different, whether we share blood or not. We're all one, connected." She shook her head. "It's a pity we don't better understand the Oldtongue word *Ahava*—to love. Because that's what we're here for. Human beings were made to love each other, to care for each other."

I remembered how, one night when I couldn't sleep, I had rested my forehead against my windowpane and watched Moish, the Watcher, out in the street.

My warm breath had misted the glass. I was about to wipe it off with my hand, but instead, on an impulse, I drew a word in the mist with my fingertip: AHAVA. It seemed to fit how I felt about Moish. And how he felt about us.

On another impulse, I had wiped the first two letters away, leaving a very different word:

AVA.

40

The sky had paled to the color of pearl, and the birds were chattering madly in the trees. I saw a flicker in the distance that I knew was Moish's campfire.

"There they are!"

My mother's eyes followed the direction of my finger. She broke into a run. I trotted along behind her, anxious to see her reunion with my father. I knew it would be so, so sweet.

A doolf appeared in our path. With hackles raised. Red eyes gleaming. Teeth bared.

I froze.

Moish materialized. Huge, powerful Moish, who had once saved me from a doolf, had arrived in time to do it again!

He growled at the beast. And the doolf *sat*. It let its tongue loll, and it wagged its tail as Moish scratched between its ears.

I stared at Moish, my mouth agape. He gave me the enigmatic smile that meant, *Have patience.*

♦

I walked on his right to the campsite. The doolf walked on his left. Still unnerved, I kept glancing over at the beast, checking it out.

There was something about it … about the way its head bobbed as it loped along. About the little patch of white on its neck.

"Hey … don't I know you?" I said to the doolf.

The doolf turned its lupine face to me. Its eyes narrowed.

The next thing I knew, it had its huge front paws on my chest. Tail wagging furiously, it was licking my face.

This doolf was the very same doolf I had looked after when it was a puppy!

41

My parents' reunion was as honey-sweet as I'd imagined. They hugged and kissed, and hugged some more. My mother hugged and kissed Dalil too.

"Thank you for everything. It's so good to have you back," she said.

"It's good to be back," Dalil replied shyly. She had the decency, at least, to look ashamed.

"Sit, make yourselves comfortable." My father swept his hand to indicate a strange clay-like structure. A shelter.

I crawled into it. It was warm and dry. "Where did this come from?"

"Thank Moish. He's part of the earth. He can communicate with it and its creatures. He asked them to help us."

"Them?" I said.

"Yes. Them. You already know that he called the doolves, right? Your 'little' friend there? But that wasn't all he did. Moish? Show Dany and Rachel."

Moish stamped on the ground. Once, twice, three times.

"Uh-oh, here it comes," Dalil said, her eyes sparkling.

I didn't know what they expected to happen, but they looked giggly. Moish too.

Nothing happened. Or so I thought.

But then I heard an eerie, whispery sound. A *chewing* sound?

I peered closer. The ground was swarming with insects. Crawling, creeping, chewing insects.

"Ugh! Gross!"

The Gol laughed.

"Moish also called the termites," my father said. "Those are the fellows that built our shelter. You should thank them."

I gave a little, creeped-out salute to the squirming mass at my feet. "Er, thank you."

My mother curtseyed. "Thank you. But please stay out of my house!"

I heard another whisper—can insects laugh?

The termites disappeared into the ground.

"Whew. That was weird," I said.

"Welcome to weird world," Dalil replied.

42

"I can't believe I'm back with this guy," I said, stroking the doolf's head. "The one silver lining in this whole mess. Khan. That's what I used to call him when he was just a pup."

Dalil snorted. "What kind of name is that? It sounds like you're clearing your throat."

"It means 'king' or 'leader' in Oldtongue," I said.

"Oh." She continued studying her fingernails as if the meaning of life were written on them.

"Our people have been using Oldtongue for generations, dear," my mother said. "You'd think growing up in a family of alchemists, you would have picked some up along the way."

I lowered my face to hide my grin. So maybe the desire for payback wasn't the most noble of emotions. But still, it was fun to see Dalil get dissed. By my *mom*.

Moish, meanwhile, stood guard over us, alert and still. He'd been like that for hours, waiting and watching. But he was getting antsy. He raised his nose to the air. His shoulders twitched. He paced.

Something was wrong.

He whistled, and Khan sprang to his side.

Moish fixed us all with a hard, red stare.

Stay right here. Don't move.

Moish and Khan jogged off together, toward Gottika.

We watched them go, our hearts in our mouths.

A few minutes passed.

I felt as twitchy as Moish.

I made a decision: no more waiting.

I pretended I was going to pee. But instead, I went to Gottika.

43

In front of the castle, a Stoon mob was facing off against the Militia. The Stoons were shouting and waving home-made weapons. Crude, yes, but good enough to deliver a solid blow.

Out of the corner of my eye, I saw Beano, a frantic expression on his face. "Ava!" he was shouting. "Ava! Where are you?" I called to him, but he didn't hear me and disappeared into the crowd.

A trumpet blared. Criers with speaker-horns shouted, "Leave now! Go back to your homes!"

Instead, the Stoons surged.

Metal and wood clashed.

Moish's instinct—his reason for existing—was to protect the Stoon people. And here were Stoons being attacked by the Militia before his very eyes.

Moish leapt into the fray, swinging his huge arms, knocking any guard who came in range to the ground. He seized guard after guard and tossed them over his shoulder. He was like an enraged child throwing his toys. And he was unstoppable.

Then things got muddy. Maybe Moish got confused by the chaos. Or by the fact that the Stoons were no longer acting the victim, but had become the aggressor. Maybe he just went crazy. But the next thing I knew, Moish was no longer our defender.

Guard, Stoon, bystander—it didn't matter. Anyone, everyone, who crossed his path was fair game.

I dashed into the crowd.

"Moish! Moish! What in God's name are you doing?"

He turned toward me, eyes flashing crimson, fist raised.

The roar of battle died on his lips. The light in his eyes dimmed. He dropped his fist.

I tugged at his sleeve. "Come on. We've got to get you out of here!"

I whistled for Khan. "Here, boy!"

We fled.

44

When Moish and I arrived back at the campsite, a hunk of venison was crackling on a spit. A basket of tiny wild strawberries overflowed onto a tarp, and two dripping chunks of honeycomb, wrapped in a burdock leaf, lay beside it.

My mother pressed me to her. "Thank God you're safe. Why did you take off like that? Without saying even a word to us?"

"I followed Moish. To the city." I reached for a chunk of meat and some honey. "I knew you wouldn't let me go if I told you. So I didn't." I swallowed noisily, and took another big bite of meat. "Where the heck did all this food come from? It's awesome."

"Two doolves brought the deer carcass," my father said.

"A bear brought the berries and honey," my mother said.

I gawked at her. "A bear? A *real* bear?"

"Indeed. He was very polite too. Though he could have used a bath. You should have told us where you were going. We were beside ourselves when you … disappeared." My mother's eyes filled with tears.

"I'm sorry," I said, giving her a hug. "I didn't mean to frighten you. But I had to go. And it's a good thing I did."

I described what had happened.

"It's like Moish just ... lost it. With everybody fighting, maybe he got mixed up. We're lucky he didn't kill anyone."

Moish bowed his head in shame.

My father sighed a deep, sad sigh. "How do you defend against violence when the people you are protecting have become violent themselves?" He stretched out a comforting hand to the Gol but hesitated and, in the end, withdrew it. "There are no easy answers in this life, are there?"

My mother clutched at her throat. "We must do something! We have to let the rest of the Stoons know you are safe so this madness will stop!"

Dalil shuddered. "No! You can't. That would be Uncle's death sentence. Trust me: I know Pol. He'll never let this drop."

My mother's face took on a new look—a determined one. "Then we must enlist Count Rayn."

"To do what?" Dalil said.

"I have an idea. But on that score, Dalil, *you'll* have to trust *me*." My mother got to her feet. "You and Judah wait here. Dany?"

She held out her hand to me.

"Let's do it," I said. "Whatever *it* is."

45

Count Rayn's face glowed with pleasure.

"It's been too long since I've seen you, my dear!" He cocked one eyebrow at me. "You know your mother and I were classmates, eh? A ridiculously long time ago. A lifetime ago. It's a pity you didn't keep up with your University studies, Rachel. You were such a dazzling student."

It's not like she had a choice, I thought.

Count Rayn's face rearranged itself into solemnity. "I heard about this business with your husband. Just terrible."

My mother bowed her head. "Then you'll be relieved to hear he's safe."

Both of Count Rayn's eyebrows shot up. "Yes? Ah. That's good news indeed. Very good news."

"Friends secured his release from the dungeons. In secret."

"I see. It's good to have friends."

My mother smiled sweetly at the Count. "Yes, it is, my old friend. Who else can you rely on, in the end?"

His mouth twitched.

She continued, "It's only a matter of time before they

147

come for us. You know my husband's innocent. I was—
am—hoping you could help us."

"Ah. Well. If only I could ... old times' sake and all that.
But my hands are tied. Look what I received today."

He withdrew a letter from his sleeve and handed it to
her. "Go ahead, read it, if you think you can stomach it.
It accuses me of plotting with your husband to kidnap
Princess Avivia. It's not signed, but I think we both know
who's behind it."

"Pol!" My mother spat the name.

"If I do anything to help you, my life will be forfeit. I
can't risk that. I have ... responsibilities. To my people."

My mother's eyes flashed. "Your people? Are not *all*
Gottikans your people? You believed in justice back in the
old days. Or were you just pretending?"

Count Rayn turned away. "I can't help you, Madame
Haleoni. I'm sorry. God be with you."

My mother's hands tightened into fists—I could see
her knuckles turn white. Her eyes became the eyes of an
avenging angel. She pointed one long, quivering finger at
Count Rayn.

"What do you know of God? How dare you speak of
him! You ... you ... you're a coward!"

Count Rayn's eyes now burned with anger. And
something else.

"So what does that make you, Rachel? You ... who've let
Pol's lies fester for all these years, because you were afraid
to speak the truth!"

148

My mother's entire body shook. She turned on her heel and stormed out.

I ran after her. I could hear the Count's shouts, echoing off the Great Room's mirrored walls. "If *you* wouldn't speak for your people, Rachel, why, then, should I?"

46

My mother's state of mind was evident in every angle of her body: the sharp swing of her elbows, her short jabbing stride.

I grabbed her arm. "Mom? Mom! What's going on? What was Count Rayn talking about?"

She shrugged my hand away and kept walking. Her lips were a thin, grim line.

I reached for her again. This time with enough force to spin her toward me.

"You've got to tell me what's going on!"

She pushed me away. "Leave me alone, Dany. This has nothing to do with you."

"It has everything to do with me! Why do all of you do this? Try to hide from the truth?"

She didn't answer me, nor slow her pace.

I shouted after her. "If you stopped trying to cover up the truth with lies and silence, everything would get better!"

She kept walking, leaving me behind.

"Wouldn't it?" I said, to no one but myself.

47

It wasn't safe to travel toward the borderlands at night. Although we were all itchy to get going, we agreed to delay our departure until after dawn, and travel with the rising sun.

Time passed slowly, the way it does at night when you cannot sleep. I spent some of it stroking Khan's thick fur. But most of it just staring at the river.

Something had to change. But I didn't know what. Or who.

When the sun rose, I rose too. All was quiet. Dalil was down by the river, washing. Moish and Khan were by the road, standing guard. My parents sat beside each other on a log, sipping cocolat. Wordlessly, I took a cup from my mother. When I'd drained it, I knew the time had come for me to speak.

"Mom? Dad? You promised me a gift when I became an adult. That's today. My thirteenth birthday."

My father looked up quickly and smiled. Deep crinkles formed at the corners of his eyes. My mother merely looked the other way.

"So it is. It's hard to believe! Only yesterday you were a toddler pretending to shave with the soapsuds in your bath."

My father reached into the collar of his shirt and lifted a gold chain off his skin. He slipped the pendant from his neck and placed it around mine. When the chain brushed my hair it felt like the gentlest of kisses.

"This is the present I promised you," he said, getting to his feet. "It's called a *maz*, and it's a magical amulet. Inside it is a sacred bit of parchment, inscribed with the holy words of God. You can turn to them in a moment of need, and they will help you."

I fumbled for words. "I … I …"

"Let me summarize what it says." He swept his arm at the horizon. "Look around you, Dany. The trees and the light, the soil beneath your feet and the sinew of your fingers—they are all shards of a primordial jug that broke at the beginning of time, creating time and space. Creating everything! The very essence of the universe is brokenness. That's why we're here."

"Huh?"

"It's our mission to help God repair it. The broken jug. The broken universe."

A bark of disbelief escaped my lips. "Oh, come on. How can we 'fix' the universe? We can't even go outdoors without a freaking hat!"

My father held up one finger. "Perhaps it does sound strange. But it's true nevertheless. The proof can be found in the Kumasha, our holiest book. In it, there's a story about creation. It tells how God literally *spoke* the world into being.

"There's a second clue. It comes from the story of Adam, the first human being. He was given the power of speech, the power of calling things by their names, of speaking the truth about their essences. Do you remember it?"

I gave a curt nod.

"It's how we become like God, Dany. Like Adam, through the gift of speech. And it's through speech that we can repair the world."

"Big deal—we can talk. That doesn't mean we have a mission. Or that we want one, either," I said.

My father reached for the pendant at my throat. He opened it. Inside, there was a tiny slip of parchment covered with minuscule, cryptic writing. He pressed the parchment into my hand and closed my fingers around it. The warm goatskin seemed to throb in time with my heart. "Doesn't matter," he said. "We've got one."

I studied the fine writing, turning the parchment this way and that, struggling to make out the words. "I can't read it."

"You'll be able to. When you need to."

It all sounded like so much nonsense. But my father, I knew, was a man of sense.

I flipped the parchment over. There were four more letters on the back: four Oldtongue letters. The same letters as on Moish's forehead?

I peered closer. No, they were similar, but not the same.

I showed the letters to my father. "What does this say?"

"Ah. That's the greatest magic of all. The secret name of God. The unnameable."

With effort, I tried to sound the word out.

"Eeahoohahhhh …"

"No, no, Dany, don't even try. The name can't be read. It can't even be spoken. But in truth it's being said, right here, right now. You can hear it, once you know how to listen."

"Come on, Dad! What's that supposed to—"

"Shhh! Just listen!"

I strained my ears, struggling to hear what my father wanted me to hear. I picked up nothing but the ordinary sounds of insects and birds, of water rushing.

I started to tell him so, but my father put his finger to his lips.

He closed his eyes. Inhaled deeply. Deeper, deeper … until his chest rose with the fullness of morning.

What the heck … why not give it a whirl? I closed my eyes and took a deep breath.

In … in … in.

When my father exhaled, I did too. Out … out … out.

Over and over again, I aped his breaths.

In. Out.

In. Out.

In. Out.

The sound of the rushing water, of the insects' chirps, faded, until there was nothing but the sound of my own breathing.

In—*Eeah*.

Out—*Hahhhh.*
In—*Eeah.*
Out—*Hahhhh.*
Eeah … Hahhhh … Eeah … Hahhhh …
Breath had become song.

I listened harder, striving to make out the melody. I only heard the steady rhythm of my mother's breath. The Gol's slow, even breaths. The doolf's panting breaths.

My soul expanded with breath. Breath was everywhere—within me, beside me, around me. The trees. The insects. The water. All breathing the same rhythm.

Could that be it? Could *this* be what I was supposed to hear?

I opened my eyes. Everything glowed with supernatural beauty. The shining face of my mother. The brilliant gleam of the water. Even the sharp skyline of Gottika City on the horizon.

I was mute with awe. I felt like I'd never really been able to *see* before. Everything, everywhere, glittered. The water shimmered, alive and sparkling. The dew gleamed on the grass, on the fresh new buds.

How could I have been so clueless?

For my whole life, the "thing" I'd been missing—that piece of the puzzle that would make my life feel like it was actually worth something—was literally *inside* me. In my mouth and heart. In the rise and fall of my own ribs.

The secret name of God. Hey, it's not much of a secret once you realize what it is. *The sound of your own breathing.*

Uh, duh.

Go ahead—say the name. Breathe in. Now breathe out.

There. You prayed. Hallelujah, Amen, bring out the party trays.

♦

Once I understood that the holiest thing of all is breath—life—I understood the flip side. Our "mission," as my dad put it.

That anyone who seeks to destroy life must be stopped.

In my mind, there was this big fat arrow pointing at Count Pol.

And another, smaller arrow pointing at me.

Oh lucky, lucky me.

PART V

"Falsehood has no feet."
—Babylonian Talmud, Shabbos 104a

48

Before I could save the world, I had to sort things out with my mother. I hunkered down in front of her and pinned her with my eyes.

"Mom, you have to tell me now." The amulet's weight pressed against my heart. "What did Count Rayn mean about letting lies fester and that you didn't speak out for your people?"

Dalil looked up sharply. This was something she wanted to hear too.

I glanced at my father. His face was unreadable.

My mother twisted her wedding ring round and round on her finger.

She whispered, "I didn't want anyone to ever know ..."

Shame etched lines into her face, sagged her shoulders.

What could my mother have done to make her feel so wretched? What did she have to be ashamed of?

She was a good, decent, honorable woman.

Wasn't she?

I was suddenly afraid. Maybe I'd opened a strongbox that should have stayed locked.

Let it drop, I told myself. *Change the subject, before it's too late.*

There was no going back. It was time to know the truth.

As if she'd heard my thoughts, my mother said, "You're right. There's no place anymore in our lives for secrets. I will tell you. All of you.

"It goes back a long way. I was just a girl. My father had been widowed when I was eight, but you know that. But this I never told any of you—no, not even you, Judah. By the time we met it was ancient histo—"

"I'm sure it wouldn't have mattered," my father said. More gruffly than I would have expected.

My mother gave him a half-smile. "Perhaps you'll think differently once I've finished. You see, my father had remarried. Just before my own thirteenth birthday."

Dalil let out a soft whistle. "You suddenly had a wicked stepmother."

"No, not wicked in the slightest. Just ..." My mother furrowed her brow. "Stiff. Maybe a bit straitlaced. But she was all right. I liked her well enough. As much as I could, anyway.

"Lilita—that was her name—had also been married before. She had a child too. A son. Suddenly, I got what I'd always wanted—what every Stoon child wants—a sib! And my new sib was a handsome fourteen-year-old boy, with the worldly ways of someone who hadn't been raised in the Stews, but had lived as a free Prahan, like his father.

"Naturally I adored Jacob. I *worshipped* him, the way any little girl would worship a handsome, suave, and sophisticated big brother. The problems started when he brought me roses ..."

Her words faltered. I could see the tips of her ears turn red.

She took a deep, steadying breath. "I was shocked—I considered him my brother, not a *boy*. Of course I couldn't go to the Spring Dance with him! That would be, just ... *weird*. Beyond embarrassing! But he didn't understand that was how I saw it. In his mind, I wasn't related to him at all. So when I recoiled, and accidentally knocked his fancy bouquet to the floor, he thought I was rejecting him. As a person."

Dalil wrapped her fingers around my mother's, but my mother didn't seem to notice. She had turned inward, watching that long-ago drama play out before her on an internal stage. Everything else here, now, had dropped away.

"I still remember the bitter words he hurled at me as if it were yesterday. 'You and your idiotic Stoon customs! Why did I ever waste my time on you?' he said. Jacob slammed out of the house. From the street below, he bellowed up at my window, 'You little Jezebel!' I didn't know what the word meant, only that it was something awful, shameful.

"He didn't see the carriage coming. There was no time for it to stop. The horses reared ...

"It was awful, too awful for words. The left side of his body—crushed. Jacob was unconscious for a week. The doctors managed to save his leg, though they said he'd always

163

walk with a limp. But his left eye … There was nothing they could do. He would never regain full vision in it.

"He refused to see me. To see any of us. Even his own mother. One day he vanished. The doctors told us he'd checked himself out of the hospice. We had no idea where he'd disappeared to, what he'd do. Lilita was beside herself with worry.

"We were at the dinner table when his letter arrived. My father read it out to us. In it, Jacob said he was with his Aunt Isabela in Ukraia.

"My stepmother gripped her wineglass so tightly it shattered in her hand. 'No! Not Isabela!' she cried out.

"'Who's Isabela?' I asked.

"Lilita replied, 'My first husband's sister. She tried to stop him from marrying me. She said my Stoon blood stank like a wild pig.'

"When my father suggested we tend to Lilita's hand and read the rest of the letter later, she said, 'No—just read.'

"She had wrapped her injured hand in her napkin. My father looked doubtful. No, not doubtful—*horrified*. But he did as Lilita asked and continued to read:

"'If only, Mother, you hadn't kept my wonderful Aunt Isabela from me all these years! It's yet another sin I lay at your feet. Now that she and I are blessedly reunited, she vows to help me regain what is mine. She says that with Father and Grandfather dead, there's no one left who knows of my Stoon taint, so I can now assume my rightful place as heir.'

"I didn't understand Jacob's letter, but it still scared me. 'Taint'—that had to be bad. I searched their faces for answers. 'What? What's going on? What's he talking about?' I asked.

"My stepmother was pinching the bridge of her nose. 'I can't believe this. He seemed so happy here,' she said.

"My father told her not to worry. He said the accident had made Jacob bitter, that it was to be expected, and that he'd get over it as he healed.

"I wasn't so sure. I knew what was really eating at Jacob. What had hurt him even more than the accident.

"Me, of course. It was me who had sent Jacob flying into the path of that carriage. Me who had caused him to lose his eye. Me who had made him turn against us.

"I thought I would die of shame. Because it was me who had turned my brother, Jacob, against our own people."

49

"No, it wasn't! It was nobody's fault! Things sometimes happen. Misunderstandings …" I said.

Dalil put her arm around my mother's shoulder. "Dany is right. Of course it wasn't your fault."

My mother placed her hand on top of Dalil's and patted it. "The story isn't over. Let's see if you still believe that when it is.

"After Jacob went to Ukraia, he turned into a different person. He renounced everything he considered Stoon, even his name. He took a new one, the name of one of his Ukraian ancestors: Pol the Implacable."

My father jumped to his feet. "Pol! You can't mean—!"

My mother lowered her eyes and twisted her wedding ring round and round.

Dalil gasped. "Of course … the mask he always wears … and the walking stick … and that one strange shoe of his …"

My father tore at his hair.

"How could you do this to me? All these years! From day one, you've been deceiving me!"

My mother shrank under the intensity of his anger.

"I never lied!" Her voice was choked with tears. "I swear, I never meant to hurt hi—you. And I never told anyone!"

I remembered the odd look that had passed between my mother and Count Rayn.

"That's not true, Mom. You *did* tell someone. Count Rayn. That's why he said what he did. He knew about Pol. And you."

My mother's eyes flashed.

"I never told him! He pieced it together for himself."

My father raged. "This is all your fault!"

Moish heard the commotion. He came running over. He looked from my father to my mother and back again, unsure of what to do. Just as I was.

"If you'd told me about your history with Pol, everything you knew about him, we could have stopped him before things went so far. We could have shown the world his hypocrisy. But now? It's too late. For us. For them. For everybody." My father made a wordless sound of disgust. "Why am I wasting my breath? I'm … I'm … finished."

He turned his back on her and walked away.

"Judah! Wait! Don't go!"

"I have to be alone for a bit. To think. To figure out who I've been living with all this time."

My mother held out her hands. "Don't you see? I couldn't expose him like that! I couldn't betray him …" Her voice dropped to a whisper. "… again."

The face my father turned to her was a blank mask.

"Even as he betrays you?" he said coldly. "Betrays all of us?"

"If only I could make you understand …"

I couldn't take it. I squeezed my eyes closed, pressed my hands over my ears, and yelled, "*Stop!* Can't you two see what you are doing to us?"

50

For years and years, nobody in my family talked about anything real. Just "Pass the potatoes" or "Watch you're not late for school again." I thought that was a nightmare.

But I was wrong. This—my mother in tears, my father raging—*this* was a nightmare.

I had to do something. I had to get my father to see how hard this whole situation was on my mother, and how little it had to do with him. But what did I know about the dynamics of love? How would I feel if I'd learned the person I loved had kept such important secrets from me?

I didn't know.

I didn't know what to say to my father, either, but I had to say something. So I went to him on the riverbank, where he sat alone.

My father looked gutted.

"Papa."

He kept his head down.

"*Papa.*"

He looked up wearily. His lips tried to form a smile but could not.

"Give her a chance, Papa. It wasn't her fault. You shouldn't blame her for another person's actions. Plus, she's your wife. Your wife! She's been living with this nightmare for a long time. Go to her. Listen to her. She needs you."

He shook his head. "Mind your own business, Dany."

I returned to the shelter. Inside it, my mother was whispering with Dalil. Dalil shot me a "not now" look. I backed away from them too.

I felt totally useless. My family was in ruins, and there was nothing I could do to repair it.

I sat on the log and stared into the heart of the fire. The flames wavered and stretched, twirled and danced.

Maybe I fell into a trance, or a dream. The flames assumed new shapes—unicorns and tiaras, demons and masks and laughing mouths. The harder I stared, the more I saw: shapes turning into letters that formed and unformed, formed and unformed.

Without my willing it, my left hand reached for the amulet around my neck. I wrapped my fingers tightly around it and again felt its mysterious pulse.

The letters kept forming and unforming in the fire. Alpha and omega, yin and yang, *hey* and *vov* and *yud*, all growing from seed-like sparks, blossoming and fading into smoke, until the cycle renewed itself.

Deep in my heart, I knew what the letters spelled.

I looked up from the flames. My eyes met Moish's across the fire.

51

I said to the Gol, "If anyone comes looking for me, tell them I went to the castle. To see Count Pol."

Dalil emerged from the termites' shelter, wiping her hands on her skirt. "Don't be a fool, Dany."

"Too late for that." I started to walk away.

My mother came out of the shelter and stood beside Dalil.

"What do you think you can say that will stop him?" my mother called to me.

"I don't know," I said over my shoulder.

Dalil ran up beside me, her breath quick and shallow.

"Your mother's right, you know. It is pointless. Pol's hardened his heart. No one can melt it now. I doubt even God himself could do it."

"Maybe. But still. Someone has to try. *I* have to try."

I stared into my cousin's eyes, as hard and defiant as my own.

"In that case, I'll come with you. I know the secret way in."

She matched her stride to mine.

A moment later, Moish and Khan joined us.

My mother gathered up her skirts, ready to run after me. "Dany! Stop!"

My father stepped into her path. "Leave him be, Rachel. Dany is a man now. He must make his own choices. Find his own way. Where we have failed, maybe Dany will succeed."

My last glimpse was of them hanging on to each other as if for dear life.

52

We went to the city. We forged our way through the roiling crowds to the castle, and slunk round to the quieter side, where the kitchens were, Dalil used her charmed key to reveal, and then open, the secret door.

Dalil led us through the castle's underground labyrinth.

We crept in single file, knowing there'd be no retreat. Every footfall echoed. The air was close—I couldn't take a full breath. Maybe I was being strangled by my own fear, my own hope.

The tunnel ended at a heavy wooden door. Dalil held up her hand. Her fingertip glowed green. Murmuring an incantation, she touched her finger to the lock. It fell to the ground with a dull *clank*. The door swung open.

On the other side, a winding staircase rose into the gloom. "There's a secret entrance to Pol's private chambers at the top," Dalil whispered. "I'll wait for you here. Be safe, my little cousin."

I kissed her on the cheek. "Thanks."

I clutched the amulet tightly in my fist and said a prayer.

Then, with Khan at my side and the Gol behind me, I went up the stairs.

I slid the door at the top open, just a bit. Through the gap, I could see Count Pol lounging on a gold silk divan. He wasn't wearing his mask. Without it, the ruins of his once-handsome face—the damaged eye, the livid scars—were plainly visible.

My mom had scars, too, only you couldn't see hers.

With my elbow, I shoved the secret panel open. Two short strides took me to him. "Hello, my uncle," I said.

He reared back in alarm. "Guards! Guards!" he shouted.

Two armed sentries rushed in. I didn't move a muscle. I didn't have to. Moish, at my side, towered over them. Khan crouched at my feet, ready to pounce.

I didn't take my eyes from Pol. Not when the clash and clang of swords rang out. Not at the guards' screams when Moish flung them to the ground.

Pol, too, was unmoved.

"Ah. Daniel, is it? A pleasure to make your acquaintance, I'm sure." A fleeting grimace further distorted his ruined face. "So your mother speaks at last?"

"Yes. She told us everything. Her secret, your secret. They're out in the open. Now it's my turn to speak. To tell you to stop this madness."

Pol threw back his head. He laughed long and loud, from deep in his gut.

"You little *pipski*. How you amuse me! You know, you're a lot like your mother, of soon-to-be blessed memory. You have her smug arrogance. Did you really think you could order me about? You? A mere child, and a Stoon at that? Did you honestly believe you'd make your childish demands and I'd say, 'Oh silly me! Sorry, people of Gottika, this Stoon hatred was just a prank!'? Or that on your say-so I'd decree the Stoons are our brothers, kind and good ..." Pol shot a glance at Moish. "Like that monster of yours. What did your 'good' father do, by the way? Conjure Samson from his grave?"

A nasty grin spread across Pol's face. "Let me ask you this, Daniel. Imagine that I could stop the Gottikan people from venting their hatred on you. Even if I could, *why would I?* You larvs, after all, are the same people who wouldn't let me into your little club, who scorned me for my mixed parentage."

"That's not what happened!"

"Oh, it isn't?" Spittle flew from his twisted lips. "Did your precious Mumsy tell you a different story? What makes you so sure I'm lying, and not *her*? This is *my* truth, nephew: Your people despised my Gottikan side. You despised it, despised me, and you threw me out. So I learned, from you, to despise my Stoon-ness. And I learned my lesson well.

"I can't remove the Stoon-ness from my body. But I *can* remove this disease from Gottika, and purify the city once and for all."

He plucked a dagger from his belt. The dark twinkle of insanity flared in his eyes. He sprang to his feet and loomed over me like a mad angel of destruction.

53

The door burst open. Guards poured through. Pol leapt onto the couch and grabbed me around the neck. "Come, my little one, your parents are waiting to greet you!" I looked to Moish for help, but he was knee-deep in guards. Ten, twenty, fifty strong … They just kept coming.

I was on my own.

I fought, I bit, I kicked, but Pol held me fast. He had size, experience, and the power of madness on his side. He dragged me to the window. I felt his dagger at my throat and his rancid breath in my ear.

"You didn't really think you were alone in that forest, did you? With all my soldiers and doolves to keep watch over you?" He smashed my face against the windowsill. The pain blinded me, but not before I'd glimpsed my mother and father in the courtyard below.

They were bound and gagged.

Pol's breath was hot on my neck. "Even your little 'friend'—yes, that doolf cowering by your feet—is with me. Didn't you wonder why he didn't leap to your defense when I took you in my arms just now? It's because he owes his true allegiance to me!

"Shiva!" Pol called to Khan. "Shiva! Come!"

Khan's ears flattened against his skull. He growled, his low, warning growl.

"Shiva! Do as I command. *Come!*"

The doolf's head bobbed back and forth. His eyes flashed red.

"No, Khan!" I yelled.

Khan leapt.

Pol's knife clattered on the floor as Khan knocked him to the ground.

The knife lay gleaming on the polished hardwood, only inches away from Pol's hand. I had to reach it before he did!

I flung myself into the fray. Pol's fingers stretched for the dagger. I batted them away and lunged for the blade.

Pol's fingers clawed at mine. They got a grip on the handle. He jackknifed to his feet, pushed Khan aside, and waggled the dagger at me.

"You may choose your last dance, Dany boy—at the end of my blade, or at the end of the long journey down!"

He forced me through the open window. Farther and farther. Pol had only to give me one more shove and I'd plummet to the stones below.

The secret door creaked. *Dalil!*

Dalil flung herself upon us and tore at Pol with her fingernails. "Leave Dany alone! You've destroyed too many lives already!"

She gripped him to her, with all her might. But even with Dalil clinging to his neck, Pol kept the upper hand. Inch by inch, he levered me through the gap.

I dangled out the window. Dalil and Pol, too, swayed precariously over empty air. In the courtyard below, doolves bayed. My parents' faces were circles of horror as they watched.

Dalil wound herself more tightly around Pol. With supernatural strength, she hauled us back in. Pol was forced to release his grip on me to fight off Dalil. They wrestled on that brink for what seemed a lifetime.

"I could have loved you," Dalil said, and pushed.

Pol's mouth contorted into a twisted O. His bony fingers scrabbled at me, at Dalil, at the window frame. They found nothing but broken glass.

His fingers slipped from the ledge. Count Pol disappeared, falling into the abyss.

I collapsed to the floor with relief. Dalil's delicate frame, however, still wavered on the windowsill, balancing on one pointed toe. With her arms outstretched and her head held high, she looked like a twinkling star poised on the lip of heaven.

Dalil shifted her weight. She reached out to empty space. Courting it. Embracing it.

I realized what she meant to do.

"Dalil!" I screamed. "No!"

She kicked out at me. "Let me go, Dany! I can't return to my old life. I don't belong there anymore."

"You don't have to do this, Dalil!" I grasped her more firmly. I knew the moment I let go, Dalil would fall. But if I didn't release her, I'd go over too.

There we were, just one heartbeat, one held breath, from eternity. Time slowed.

Dalil's fragile balance shifted. She was flailing, failing, falling …

My own toes left the ground. We were going over!

Moish yanked me back. He held on to me, even as I cried out. Even as my cousin slipped through my fingers like sand, like water.

Did I really see, then, what I think I saw?

Dalil's body spun out, out, out, into the darkness. But she didn't fall. Instead, she burst into flame, like a shooting star.

For a single, sparkling moment, I saw her outline, etched with diamonds, hovering in the air. A crown of gold adorned her head. The shimmering diamonds faded, and Dalil was gone.

54

Does it sound childish to say I burst into tears? Well, if it does, too bad.

I buried my face in Khan's warm fur and cried like a baby. He nipped at me. He whined, and nipped again.

I looked into Khan's eyes.

"What is it, boy? What do you want?"

He whined again and nudged my cheek with his snout.

I looked over my shoulder. Behind me stood a wooden chest.

"Is there something in the chest, Khan?"

In reply, the doolf heaved himself toward it.

I crawled to the chest. I unfastened its clasps. My hands were sore and shaking, making me clumsy beyond words. But I had to open that chest—Khan was trying to tell me something about it, something important. I had to see what was inside.

I freed the latches. I pushed the heavy lid up.

Inside was a girl.

She looked dead.

I touched the body to make sure.

The flesh was cool. But, wait … there was the very faintest pulse.

Before I was even able to call his name, Moish was at my side.

Together, we lifted the unconscious girl from the strongbox. We carried her to the divan and placed her gently onto the silk cushions.

Guards swept into the room. I ignored them.

I brushed the damp hair away from the girl's face. "It's Ava!" I breathed.

At the same instant, a startled guard gasped, "It's the Princess Avivia!"

The girl's eyelids fluttered, and she opened her eyes.

"Dany? Is that you?"

I was quaking, so stunned I could barely speak. "Are you—? I mean, who are you—I mean—God, I don't know what I mean. I'm just glad you're safe."

I gave her water to drink. When the color returned to her face, and she was able to sit up, I asked her what had happened.

"I don't know." Her brow creased. "One minute I was sitting in the library, working on my lab report. And the next I woke up in a speeding carriage, with a blindfold over my eyes and a wicked headache. After that, it's a blur. And then—nothing."

There was a commotion at the door. My mother and father! Someone had freed them!

"My darling boys! Thank God you are both safe!" My mother hugged me, then Moish, then both of us together.

"Mom, Papa. There's someone here you need to meet. This is Beano's sister. Ava. But she goes by another name too."

55

The next day, for the second time in my life, I went to the Autumn Palace.

This time, I wasn't forced to dress in the open air. This time, I'd been brought to the palace by a gilded coach, drawn by four prancing white horses. Alone.

In the Great Room, the Queen and Princess Avivia sat next to each other on a sofa. Ava jumped to her feet and hugged me.

"I can't tell you how grateful I am to you for saving my daughter," Queen Areya said.

"You're very welcome, Your Royal Highness. But, please—if I can ask you something?"

She nodded. "Of course. Anything."

"I don't get it. Why was Princess Avivia pretending to be Beano's sister?"

The Queen sighed and patted the seat beside her. "Come. Sit."

I sat.

"Nothing is simple in life, is it?" She sighed again. "It comes down to this: I was a young mother, and I was scared.

"I'd heard about what was going on in Gottika. With people disappearing. I had an inkling, too, of who might be behind it. Not that I was the only one—many people suspected Pol was involved somehow. But I had another reason to fear him, and to fear for my own daughter's safety.

"Many years ago—Avivia was only four then, weren't you, darling?—I decided the best course of action would be to send Avivia far away, to a place where even Pol couldn't find her. I entrusted a young man to take her with him to Praha. I knew he was loyal to me, and that he had a good heart.

"Who would ever suspect that the little girl who arrived in Praha with the Stoons named Sandor and Penina was anything other than their daughter? I believed she was safe. I counted on it. But who can predict what path a life will take, especially when love is involved?"

The Queen reached into a carpetbag. She pulled out a stack of papers.

"When his wife died, Sandor knew he couldn't look after Avivia alone. He did what he thought was best. He brought Avivia to the only other person he knew would care about her and protect her as completely as he would."

The Queen spread the old, yellowed papers out on a table in front of us. I saw a number of heliographs of an identitatt. Some passage certificates.

"Look at these carefully, Dany. They are Avivia's history. They document her true identity."

I picked up one of the heliographs and read the faded script.

None of it made sense. "What is this one?" I asked, holding one sheet of crinkly parchment in the air. "It's got Mrs. Beanburg's name on it. Is this her passport?"

The penny dropped.

I gaped at Queen Areya, at Avivia, and back at the Queen.

"Those documents bear the names of Avivia's true parents. I'd adopted her, you see."

I couldn't believe what I was hearing, seeing.

"If Avivia is adopted ... and Beano's mother is her birth mother ... that means Avivia really *is* Beano's sister. The one stolen when she was a baby. When his father disappeared!"

My face grew hot. My skin prickled, and my breath caught in my throat.

"How could you? You took a newborn baby from her real mother, a mother who *grieved*, who almost died of a broken heart! Her husband never returned!"

The Queen had tears in her eyes.

"I know. I know. I was desperate for a child ... And I was young. Very young. I didn't understand then what I know now. But I can't regret having my daughter."

I turned to Avivia. "Did you know too?"

Avivia shook her head. "Not really. I knew that Sandor and Penina weren't my real Mama and Papa. But I didn't know who was. I only knew that, once in a while, this lady

185

that smelled nice and had pretty clothes used to come and play with me. In Praha."

"I missed her terribly," said the Queen. "But if Pol had found out who her real parents were ... He could have brought down the entire kingdom."

I felt my jaw tighten. "You know that you can't keep it a secret anymore. If the kingdom isn't strong enough to survive the truth, then it doesn't deserve to survive, does it?"

I turned to Avivia. "Avivia, Ava, whatever you want to call yourself—you're a Stoon. Like me. None of this—" I waved my arm at the grand furnishings around us—"changes that."

"You're right. I'm a Stoon and proud of it. And now that I know the whole truth of who I am, things are going to be different. Aren't they, Mother?"

"They already are," the Queen said. "They already are."

PART VI

"The parchments are being burnt but the letters are soaring on high."

—Babylonian Talmud, Avodah Zara 18a

56

It was evening, one of those magical, long evenings when the flowers bloom and the birds build nests and sing love songs in the bowers above your head. To my utter joy, my mother and father were talking to each other again, working to patch things up. It wasn't perfect between them yet, but it was good. Very good.

Another reason for celebration was that my father had saved the lives of the servant couple—and their son—Count Pol had locked in the castle sewers. Papa used the same spell Dalil had to open the lock. He'd promised to teach it to me too.

"I don't think there has ever been a sweeter spring than this one," my father said, taking a bite of meatball.

My mother said, "I know ... It feels like when we were young, and anything was possible."

My father said, "Even the most bigoted Gottikans can't ignore the prosperity that has come to our city since the Counts set up the new Ministry of Justice and the Stoon laws have been repealed." He unconsciously rubbed at his wrist where his Stoon identification tag had once been embedded. Only a tiny, zigzag scar remained.

I looked across at Moish. He was sitting on his low stool, not eating. He was the only one who did not seem happy.

What does a warrior do without a war? I thought.

"Mom? Papa? What about Moish?"

"What about him?"

"He's doing just fine. Leave him be," my mother said.

"But Pa—"

"You heard your mother."

57

It's the merry, merry month of May. A fine time to finally face the facts.

Moish, a man made out of prayers and clay, is the only creature in this world that is truly alone.

He's neither here nor there—neither Stoon nor Gottikan, human nor animal, flesh nor earth. He might grow, he might change, he might think, he might feel. But he will never, ever, *ever* belong.

Thinking on this just about breaks my heart.

Then there's this, a second ugly truth: Moish

—my hero

—my Gol

—my brother

has outlived his purpose.

Mom and Papa won't accept it. They think of Moish as if he were a little kid. They indulge him when he gets up to his tricks, like tearing apart the gazebo in the park or uprooting all the city's prized cherry trees.

But I've learned the hard way that lies come in many shapes and colors. And that sometimes the cruelest lies are the ones we tell ourselves.

58

I asked Moish to come with me to the Meeting House. On the way we passed Beano and Ava. She was wearing a stylish red beret. Suddenly, Stoon hats were Gottika chic.

Seeing Beano and Ava together sent a pang through my heart. They were brother and sister, flesh and blood. Moish was my brother, but he was neither flesh nor blood.

As real as he was to me, Moish was not real.

We reached the Meeting House. I commanded Khan to sit and wait at the foot of the stairs. He whined at being left alone, but once I'd given him a good scratch behind the ears, he settled down to lick his paws.

I looked up the long flight of stairs. Above the door, there was a carving of the Holy Tablets. The Oldtongue letters had been formed with magic, so that the letters were completely free, unsupported on any side by stone. A bright light shone through the letters, as if sunlight were pouring from the interior of the Meeting House and casting its rays upon the street.

Funny, I had never noticed that effect before.

Moish and I climbed the stairs and entered the building.

Here, the identical quality of light seemed to stream *in* through the letters. *Only your perspective*, they seemed to say, *has changed.*

It's the perfect metaphor, I thought. Magic working in two directions—both in and out. *Like breathing.* Who could even say where one breath began and one ended? Different but the same, both part of one whole.

We burrowed deeper into the building, along the spine of the prayer hall and up onto the dais. Behind it, a flight of stairs led to the building's attic.

We climbed the stairs, leaving our footprints in the unmarked dust.

The attic was just as dusty as the staircase. Bookcases filled with ancient tomes lined every wall, stretching up to the ceiling. They threatened to topple over at the slightest breath, but there wasn't a whisper of air. Not a single page fluttered.

For the thousandth time, I questioned my decision. Could I, *should* I do this? So what if Moish was different from everyone else? Didn't he deserve to have a life? Didn't all God's creatures? Even if they were flawed?

Yes. Absolutely yes.

But Moish wasn't God's creature. He was my father's creation. A confabulation of dust and dreams.

I told Moish to sit on the floor, with his back against the books. "Close your eyes. Rest. Your work is done."

But he wouldn't listen. His eyes grew wide. He looked … *yes, scared.*

The corners of my own eyes stung. I blinked, and blinked again, and made my voice gentle and soothing.

"Rest. Your work is done, Moish."

His eyelids closed. A few moments later, he was asleep.

I covered his bulky frame with frayed prayer shawls. When I'd tucked him in, I steeled myself for what I had to do next.

It was the right thing, I knew. But, oh, how it hurt. *It hurt.*

I wiped off the E, the first letter of the Oldtongue word EMET, from Moishe's forehead. Now it read MET. The Oldtongue word for death.

Moish's eyes flew open, burning red. His mouth gaped as if to scream, but no sound emerged, only smoke. The life force was burning him, consuming him, from within.

Tears ran freely down my cheeks. They landed with a *plunk* on the hands of the Gol.

"Ashes to ashes, dust to dust," I said, stumbling through the holy words, "… may God's illustrious name be blessed always and forever."

The fire in the Gol's eyes dimmed. The lines of his face softened. He was melting back into a lump of clay.

"Blessed, praised, glorified, exalted, extolled …" I chanted, lifting the magical amulet from around my neck, "… and acclaimed be the name of the Holy One beyond any other uttered in this world. Amen."

I removed the sacred scroll from the amulet.

This time, when I tried to read the words it contained, I was able.

Before the universe
There was nothing but
God

Grand
Formless
Singular

Alone and
Lonely

So God contracted himself
Like the iris of an eye
And a circle of emptiness opened
Inside him.

In it he created a vessel
A cosmic crucible
A heavenly amphora

And into it he breathed all
The stuff of the universe.

Too small
To contain
God's glory

It shattered.

A billion hurtling shards
Of damaged divinity
Flew into every cleft of the universe

Gave it shape
And substance.
But also evil;

For every shard
By its very nature
Has a razor's edge.

And so God created
Humanity
To gather the shards
To reunite them

To remove borders
And recreate
The shining, perfect vessel.

◆

I closed my eyes to steady myself. *Could I really do this?*

I had to.

I would.

I took a deep breath and placed the piece of parchment in my mouth. Holding it steady with my lips, I leaned forward and pressed my mouth to the Gol's. A last kiss.

I exhaled.

WooooOOOOSH! Carried by my breath, the scroll flew into the Gol's mouth.

A mighty wind rose around us. It grew stronger and stronger, swirling like a cyclone. Bits of paper, loose sheets from old books, torn parchment, scraps of ancient newspapers, all were caught up in the wind, more and more and more, until I felt myself swimming in a whirlpool of words.

At the center sat the Gol. He stared up at me, his eyes how they were on the first day: soft, vulnerable.

The light in them was fading.

I kept my own eyes locked on his, refusing to take the cowardly way out, refusing to look away.

"Goodbye, my friend. My brother," I whispered, my voice breaking.

Shards of clay flew off in all directions, like a pot exploding in a kiln.

59

Beneath the prayer shawls, the Gol lay still. Nothing more, now, than an inert, misshapen sculpture. A piece of a finger lay where it had fallen, a broken shard from a broken pot.

I covered the Gol—what was once the Gol—with books, building a temple of sorts over his body. The books, I hoped, would hide him until his empty shell crumbled to dust. I hoped it would last until even the memory of who he had been, of who *we* had been, was lost forever in the mists of time.

60

The truth is never what you expect.

Neither as wondrous nor as terrible.

Maybe because truth is just another word for life.

I've learned, too, there's no such thing as good and bad. They're just different sides of the shards. The shiny face, and the sharp edge.

You do with them what you will.